The Move

Georges Simenon

The
Move

Translated

from the French by

Christopher Sinclair-Stevenson

A Helen and Kurt Wolff Book

Harcourt, Brace & World, Inc., New York

BY WAY OF A PREFACE

Certain critics, rare it is true, certain foreign publishers used to fine big books, really thick ones, have reproached me for only writing short novels.

This one is particularly short. I could have diluted it. I would have considered myself, if I had acted in that way, guilty of cheating my readers and myself.

GEORGES SIMENON

The Move

Chapter One

I T was the second night. He had remained awake as long as possible, keeping his eyes open for a long time. Between the slats of the metallic shutters there filtered a little of the light from the two electric lamps which illuminated the street, on the far side of the lawn.

Blanche was sleeping. She had the ability to fall asleep the minute she got into bed. One might have described her as working herself into a comfortable position, like an animal. She moved about for a few moments, burrowed into the mattress, buried her head in the pillow.

"Good night, Emile. . . ."

He leaned over her, kissed her on the cheek, his lips every now and then touching a lock of hair.

"Good night, Blanche. . . ."

Five or six minutes later, moved by a vague tenderness, like a feeling of remorse, he would often murmur gently:

"Good night. . . ."

She rarely answered, and it was not long before he heard that special breathing of hers. When they were first married he used to tease her:

"Do you know you snore?"

She seemed so anxious, so worried, that he added hastily:

"It's not real snoring. Only a faint hum, like the sound of a bee in flight in the sunshine. . . ."

"It doesn't disturb you?"

"Of course not. On the contrary. . . ."

He was not lying. Generally this rhythmic hum helped him to sleep and he was surprised to find himself breathing in time to it.

That particular night he did not want to go to sleep. He was waiting, his head close to the wall. At about eleven o'clock he had heard the woman on the other side going to bed. The partition which separated the two apartments was obviously thin, or else there was some defect in the masonry at this spot, perhaps a broken brick?

She must be asleep, like the night before. Unless, like him, she was waiting.

Now and then he caught the noise of a car drawing up outside one of the units of the housing project. The sound of voices reached him. Nearly always couples. The engine was turned off. He imagined the woman looking for the key in her bag, or the man for his in his pocket. Quite soon a light would appear in a window.

He was annoyed with himself. He was ashamed. Now and then he closed his eyes, intending to let himself fall asleep, but almost at once the longing returned to him forcefully, to listen as he had done the night before.

What time was it, that night, when the man came home? He did not even know that. Afterwards he had not dared turn on the light so as to look at the time on the alarm clock. Noises, voices, laughter, then all the rest, had waked him up with a start. He was still not used to living in this building, where they were sleeping for the first time, it was inevitably so different from Rue des Francs-Bourgeois.

4

At any rate he had stayed for more than an hour with his ear pressed against the wall so as to hear better, and by the time all was silent again he was no longer altogether the same man.

The proof of this lay in the fact that, in spite of being a glutton for sleep, he was now doing his utmost to stay awake and listen again. Did it happen every night? Were his neighbors husband and wife? Or was it only an isolated visit which recurred at long intervals?

He had never seen either of them. He had no first-hand knowledge of any of the tenants in the building; he did not even have any idea of how many there were. There were at least two apartments on each of the eight stories. More than that, since the board advertised apartments containing five, four, or three rooms, not counting the studio.

There was not merely a single building; there were at least twenty, identical, grouped geometrically, with the same number of square yards of lawn in front of each, the same trees which had only just been transplanted.

He did not regret his decision. Besides, they had taken it together, Blanche and he. For about two years he had been reading in the papers advertisements for new towns which were going up in ever-increasing numbers around Paris.

"You don't think we'll feel a bit lost?"

Blanche never gave a positive opinion. She would rarely make an objection even in the form of a query. He was the man, her husband, the head of the family.

Alain, in contrast, had almost rebelled.

"What do you think I'll do in a housing development? Besides the fact that I'll have to change my school?"

"It's up to your father to decide, Alain. . . ."

"My father isn't thirteen any longer. He never goes out, except once in a blue moon to take you to the movies. He hasn't even got any friends. I have!"

5

"Once we're there you'll be able to make new ones. . . ."

"Do you know what kind of people we'll find at Fairview? It's not even the name of a district, of a town or village, just a word invented by the publicity agents. . . ."

Alain grumbled, as he did every year, about where they had decided to go on holiday.

"Dieppe again, where it rains every other day and it's nearly always too cold to swim . . . Why can't we go to Spain like all my friends?"

"Because your father doesn't get his holiday in the summer and he can only join us on weekends. . . ."

"Couldn't we go to Spain, just the two of us?"

"And leave him alone at home every Sunday?"

It was only June. Nothing had been decided. All of their time had been occupied in arranging the move.

Emile refused to sleep. He needed to listen again, but his thoughts were becoming hazier. He suddenly grudged his wife her snoring, which gradually began to dominate his own breathing. He would fall asleep without being certain of waking with a start like the previous night.

Blanche, for her part, never woke up during the night. She had no need of an alarm clock. At six o'clock, give or take a couple of minutes, she opened her eyes, slid noiselessly out of bed, and, carrying her dressing gown and slippers, went off to the kitchen.

Even when they were still living on Rue des Francs-Bourgeois she managed to shut the door again without making any noise in spite of its sagging.

It was ridiculous to wait like this for something which might not happen. He was not proud of himself. What excuse would he have given if he had been caught with his ear pressed against the partition?

He was not afraid of Blanche. She was his wife. In fifteen

years of marriage she had not reproached him even once. Nor did she ever make fun of him, however lightly, as most women did of their husbands.

Even so he was uneasy about her judgment, about an indefinable gleam which sometimes appeared in her eyes, about a look more sustained and questioning than usual.

The night before, because he was asleep, he had not heard the car until he had been wakened by the voices. Probably the man had come by car. In the morning he had noticed, parked by the curb, a cherry-red sports convertible, which stood out against the gray of most of the other cars.

Their car . . .

Everything became blurred, and when he opened his eyes it was no longer the light from the street lamps which was filtering through the shutters but the early-morning sun. He touched the bed beside him. Blanche was up, and he thought he could already catch the smell of coffee.

He felt disgruntled, irritated with himself. At one and the same time irritated at having gone to sleep and irritated at having tried to stay awake.

He should have felt happy. The walls were white, a soft white nearer ivory, without a mark, without a crack. It was no longer a case of the dreary flowered wallpapers of Rue des Francs-Bourgeois, peeling in places, or of the ones in his father's little house in Kremlin-Bicêtre.

For years, in fact all his life, he had hated flowered wallpapers which symbolized for him a certain mentality and state of mind.

He remembered one summer, when he was seven or eight. In those days young people did not rush off to the beach or go abroad.

Some did not have any holidays at all. Others went to some village where they had relatives and where the chief distraction was fishing for frogs in the ponds. Everything reeked of manure. Even the rooms. One was wakened early in the morning by the mooing of cows.

He still went once a week to Kremlin-Bicêtre on a ritual visit to his widowed father, who was now retired after forty years as a teacher. There were three small houses built of cut stone between the tenement buildings, and as soon as one pushed open the door one heard the ticking of the brass clock in the dining room.

Now the walls all around Emile were spotless, without a trace of previous occupants and their existence.

They were the first. One of the buildings, to the east, was not finished and a gigantic crane slanted its jib into the sky.

Besides the chest of drawers, the bedside table, and a small oval table, there was no other furniture in the room except for the bed, as there was no longer any need for the enormous walnut wardrobe which used to take up all the space in Rue des Francs-Bourgeois.

He had said nothing, the day before yesterday, when the bed had been installed against the wall. He had looked at the chest of drawers, a wedding present from Blanche's aunt, the bedside table, the easy chair upholstered in a dull tapestry.

Because of the move they had regretfully parted company with some pieces of furniture which had become useless or were too much of an encumbrance.

At the moment, he looked discontentedly at what they had brought with them. He hadn't yet raised the subject with Blanche. He would do so later, in a few weeks' time. She was more conservative than he, more sentimental, and he knew she would only reluctantly agree to part with their bed, for example.

To her it was the symbol of their life together, of their

8

marriage, of their love, of the birth of Alain, of their joys and their minor illnesses throughout fifteen years.

He pushed open the bathroom door. Alain was there, standing naked under the shower which was installed over the bath.

"What time is it?" the boy asked.

"Half-past six."

"Is breakfast ready?"

"I haven't been into the kitchen."

"Haven't you seen Mother?"

"Not yet."

"You know, I'd rather leave ten minutes earlier. Yesterday I got there the very moment they were going into class and only just had time to slip in at the end of the line."

"We were delayed by a heavy truck."

"There are heavy trucks every day."

Why, on the plans, did they call it a shower room instead of a bathroom? It was after all a proper bathroom, done up with dark blue tiles on the floor and the walls covered with a lighter blue, and there was no need to wait for an old gas water heater to make up its mind to function before running the bath.

He had suffered from that so-called bathroom on Rue des Francs-Bourgeois, fitted out with odds and ends, with frosted-glass windows that stopped one from seeing the courtyard, which was hardly bigger than a chimney.

All that was over, that and the racket of a working-class street which went on from early in the morning.

"We're going to lead a new life!" he had cried when they had got back from signing the papers for the new apartment.

Lead a new life! Can one ever lead a new life?

But he was not disappointed. There was nothing to make him complain, or think that he had made the wrong choice.

"If only one could see the sun for longer than a quarter of

9

an hour a day!" he had moaned for nearly fifteen years.

He saw it now. As soon as he raised the shade, the room was flooded with it. He opened the window and saw, in front of him, at least thirty yards away, a white building identical to theirs. There, too, each apartment had a concrete balcony, and on some of them washing was hanging out to dry.

Rue des Francs-Bourgeois, at the spot where they had still been living only three days earlier, was barely five yards wide and one had to get off the sidewalk when one met someone coming the other way.

Two airplanes zoomed through the sky, hidden now and again by the morning mist. They were only five miles from Orly.

"You won't be in line with the runways," the agent had assured them. "You'll only hear a slight noise and you'll quickly get used to it. All the new tenants made the same objection, and since then I haven't had a single complaint."

He had put on his blue dressing gown and was crossing what they called on the plans the living room. He did not like that word either. Shower room, living room. It was both a dining room and a sitting room, because a small wall about three feet high divided it into two parts.

Until they could get something better, they had put on it a thick-leaved plant in a copper cachepot which they had had since heaven knows when in the dining room on Rue des Francs-Bourgeois.

"Good morning, Blanche. . . ."

She held up her forehead to him, a frying pan in her hand.

"Good morning, Emile. . . . Did you sleep well? I was just about to wake you up when I heard you talking to Alain. . . . Is he ready for breakfast?"

Alain always had two fried eggs while his father made do with black coffee and occasionally a croissant. Blanche had already seen the baker and made arrangements with

10

him, so that fresh bread and croissants were left outside
their door at half-past six.

"We're going to have a fine day. . . ."

"It'll be hot," he objected.

He added without conviction:

"There'll undoubtedly be a storm in the afternoon. . . ."

He was probably wrong and he was angry with himself
for almost maliciously tarnishing in this way a morning which
promised to be radiantly fine.

Fairview! An idiotic name, which reeked of artifice, publicity, confidence games. He imagined the man charged with
finding a name for the new housing development racking his
brains.

They would have told him:

"It must be gay, full of sunshine. . . . It must conjure up
the joys of living. . . ."

There was Fairgates already, and besides there were no
gates here. Somewhere there was even a Sunshine Estates.
He could not visualize himself announcing to someone that
he lived at Sunshine Estates.

And what about Fairview?

Even if the kitchen was not a large one, everything was
perfectly appointed, straight out of an exhibition.

"Did you find the butcher?"

"He comes over every morning from Rungis. All I need
do is telephone my order. In a few months the self-service
store will have a section for meat and another section for
fish. . . ."

Alain appeared, dressed, his hair damp.

"Ready?"

"I've just got to fry your eggs."

He sat down at the varnished table, an English book in
front of him. Emile, for his part, carried through the living
room the cup of coffee his wife had just given him and made

his way toward the bathroom, stopping every now and then to take a mouthful.

Had the man and the woman on the other side of the wall got up? It was unlikely. The night before last they had not gone to sleep until three in the morning, if not later.

He gave an odd kind of smile. It was himself he was laughing at. If they went to bed in the small hours and got up in the middle of the morning, was it not likely that he would never meet them?

Consequently he wouldn't know what either of them looked like. He would know more about the intimate side of their life than one would usually know about one's best friends, about one's family, about one's wife even, but he might meet them in the street without knowing who they were.

The bathroom floor was wet; a washcloth was lying on the tiled floor. He swore at his son and was glad that, at the beginning of the autumn term, he was going to the Villejuif lycée. There would no longer be any need to drive him into Paris before eight o'clock. Alain would take the streetcar. His father wouldn't have a whole hour to kill before his office opened.

It was impossible to move the boy to a new school just when the exams were coming up. There were dozens of problems like that. They had thought of some in advance. They had seemed simple enough, easy to solve. Why should Emile suddenly worry?

To be strictly accurate, he was not worrying. Nor was he disappointed. It was like certain Sundays when he was a child. His parents used to plan excursions. For example, they would go and have lunch by the Seine and, of course, for reasons of economy, they would take a picnic lunch. They didn't own a car. They walked. They went across the sand.

"Watch out for the puddles, Emile. . . ."

He longed to do as so many others did—have some fried fish in an open-air café. The grass on which they sat was dusty and had a strange smell.

Why did they nearly always end up quarreling, sometimes before they left, sometimes in the middle of the afternoon? His mother was a nervous woman. Like Blanche, one would have said, she was afraid of her husband, when really it was he who had put up with her whims.

When they had driven up, with the moving van behind them, he was beaming with joy.

"Life is beginning, you'll see!"

"Weren't you happy before?"

"Yes, of course. But . . ."

Not the least of their pleasure lay in the fact they were at last somewhere brand-new, somewhere clean, in surroundings untarnished by other restricted lives, impregnating the walls and the floors with their disappointments, their anxieties, their unhappiness, and their illnesses.

"See how gay it is!"

As he raised his head, he had seen at a window below their apartment the bald pate of an old man with bloodshot eyes, looking lifeless already, a small pipe stuck in his mouth.

The quickest way of getting onto the throughway was to take the unpaved road under the railway bridge. One crossed the site of a building still in construction where the streets could only be guessed at; to the left, Orly Airport was visible again.

Alain, sitting beside his father in the front of the car, looked at the countryside without enthusiasm.

"What are you thinking about?"

"That I'll have to make new friends. From what I've been able to see that won't be easy."

"Aren't you glad we've left Rue des Francs-Bourgeois?"

"Why should I be glad?"

"You've got a large room now. You can have a bath or a shower every morning without waiting to see whether the water heater has made up its mind to work. Next year the swimming pool will be finished."

"Considering the number of tenants, one will have to put one's name down on a list every time one dives in."

"For your next birthday I'll buy you a motor scooter. You won't need to go to school by streetcar."

"I wonder what kind of school they could possibly have at Villejuif."

Emile Jovis felt vaguely guilty. He had not sensed any enthusiasm on the part of his wife, either. He had convinced himself that the move was for the benefit of them all and that it was going to make them happy.

Perhaps it was the same with Blanche and their son as with himself? He had no regrets. It was too soon for that. Their experience was too fresh, it had hardly lasted forty-eight hours.

What had been missing—at any rate, for Jovis—was the establishment of contact. He had imagined that their arrival in their new life would be smooth, that everything would immediately fall into place around them, that they would all be glad simultaneously to rid themselves of a dusty past.

"What is Mother going to do all day?"

He looked at his son out of the corner of his eye, surprised by the question.

"What do you mean? She'll do what she's always done."

"You think so?"

Suddenly he didn't, but even so he answered:

"What did she do in Paris? Housework, shopping, going to the market, cooking . . ."

"You won't come home for lunch any more, and I won't either when I go to the school at Villejuif. At Fairview there's only one shop. All around it's wasteland. One doesn't go for walks in wasteland."

He had always sought Alain's approbation, and it pained him not to find it this time.

"Don't you like the new apartment?"

"I've got nothing against the house."

"When your room has been properly furnished . . ."

"I spend so little time in my room!"

"This evening they'll install television."

"I know."

"Well?"

"Well nothing."

He was sulking about their new life before giving it a try. Too bad if Emile had made a mistake. It was too late to go back, because they had bought the apartment on a fifteen-year mortgage.

They left the throughway at the Porte d'Italie and were driving toward the Seine, which they crossed at the Pont d'Austerlitz. A little later, near the Saint-Paul métro station, Alain got out opposite the Lycée Charlemagne. It was five minutes to eight.

"Have you got your money?"

The boy assured him that he had it in his pocket. It was for his lunch. Problems of this sort were cropping up, like this one which had had to be worked out the evening before.

Emile could not pick up Alain again for lunch as he did not know in advance what time he would be leaving his office. Each of them would follow his own schedule.

When they were living on Rue des Francs-Bourgeois it was easy, as their house was only a few hundred yards away and the meal was waiting for them.

Yesterday Blanche had spent the day putting linen and clothes in the closets. Between the bathroom and Alain's room there was a walk-in closet with shelves on three sides.

"Think how handy that will be!" Emile had cried when they had been to see the brand-new apartment three months earlier.

The plumbers and the painters were still at work. It was difficult to estimate the size of the empty rooms, where their voices echoed strangely.

"What do you think of it?"

"It's nice," Blanche said pleasantly.

She looked around her as if to find her place in this new world.

"Your cleaning will be cut in two, because everything's so easy to keep up. Besides, there are closets everywhere."

"I must get my bearings."

The day before yesterday, while the men were bringing in the furniture, she had mistaken the door of a closet for that of the living room. It was only a question of getting used to it.

On Rue des Francs-Bourgeois, the apartment clung to their bodies like an old garment, with its accumulated smells and a patina on everything which did not date from their period of occupation but from many generations of unknown people.

Nothing functioned properly—the windows which the wind came through, the shutters with their missing hooks, the front-door bolt which could be shot only when one pulled up on the door.

Every evening the Malards, above them, watched television until eleven-thirty, and the noise was as loud as if it were in their own apartment.

In the local shops Blanche had to queue up, and listen to the gossiping of the old women who had new secrets to exchange every morning.

Jovis had an hour to kill. His office did not open until nine. He drove toward Place des Vosges and stopped the car near the corner of Rue de Turenne.

The day before, he had gone to have a cup of coffee on the terrace of the bar which stood at an angle to the street. There were only four or five little tables and a few chairs on the sidewalk. The awning was down because the sun was already hot and beating on the front of the building.

He had had time to read his paper from cover to cover. He could do the same today, and then the following days, until the scholastic year was over and he no longer had to drive his son to the Lycée Charlemagne.

The waiter was standing in front of him.

"I'll have . . ."

He hesitated, and saw on the windowpane, written in chalk by hand, the words: NEW CONSIGNMENT OF POUILLY.

"A glass of Pouilly. . . ."

He drank little, taking an apéritif only when he happened to be with friends or sometimes on a Sunday evening when he went out with Blanche and Alain. At meals he was satisfied with a glass or two of red wine.

He went to look for a paper on one of the tables inside. He had known this bistro when it was a gloomy place, with an old tin counter, sawdust on the floor, and the owner a one-armed man from the Auvergne.

The Auvergnat was dead. The new proprietor had done up the whole place, installed a brass counter, neon lighting, new tables, new chairs. Now one could have a real meal, standing up, surrounded by a variety of appetizing cold cuts.

"Is it true you've left the district?"

"Two days ago. We've moved to a new apartment about six miles from Orly."

"But you haven't changed your job? You still work near the Bastille?"

"Yes, I'm still there."

"Are you in one of those developments one can see from the throughway to the south?"

"Not a development . . ."

Because it was not shoddy. The houses were not jerry-built, they were well-finished concrete buildings with patches of green laid out between them.

The promoter must have balked at using the word "residence," as they did in the luxury places. That way, he would have run the risk of putting off the middle-income class of customer. He had simply baptized the place Fairview, without further classification.

"Does your wife like it?"

"I think so."

"She will. Women adjust more slowly than we do. When we came here, I thought for six months that my wife would become a nervous wreck. In Rue de Clignancourt she knew the whole district."

The Pouilly was fresh and dry. He drank it in nearly one gulp, and a few minutes later he felt like drinking another and made a sign to the waiter.

He had no serious reason to be preoccupied or worried. Deep down, what was bothering him was what had happened the first night on the other side of the wall, or rather the fact that he had listened right to the end, that he had been sufficiently disturbed by what he heard to make an effort to keep awake the following night.

He was ashamed. He had behaved like a voyeur. It was contrary to his character, to his convictions, to the standard of conduct which he had followed scrupulously all his life.

Up to now he had been at peace with himself, mindful of doing his best to make people happy and doing his duty toward his family and his employees.

Wasn't it ridiculous to be annoyed with himself because he had overheard some noises, voices, words which revealed a world he had not imagined existed?

18

He remembered a friend at the Kremlin-Bicêtre school where in one of the classes he had had his own father as teacher. This friend was the only boy in the class with red hair, and everyone pretended that he smelled because his father was a street-sweeper. He was bigger, more sturdily built than the others, and his face was freckled.

"Hey, you, have you ever seen your father get on top of your mother?"

Emile had blushed. He must have been eight or nine and his mother was still alive. Of course he knew that children were not brought by the stork, but his knowledge was very limited and he preferred not to find out any more.

It worried him, when he thought of his mother, to imagine certain movements which his schoolfellows whispered about.

"They don't do it," he had replied. "Otherwise I would have brothers and sisters."

The other boy had been called Ferdinand.

"Do you believe that? Well, chum, you're pretty simple! I've seen my old man and woman carrying on. I watched through the keyhole. One's parents are just like other people. To begin with, it was not my father who started, but my mother."

Emile was ashamed to listen, yet he longed to ask questions. He had finished by stammering out, hating himself as he said it:

"Was she undressed?"

"I'll say she was undressed! I was going to tell you . . ."

It was one of his worst memories, and it had taken him years, if not to forget it, at least to banish it from his mind for long periods.

When on the first evening of their marriage he had found himself alone with Blanche in a room in a Dieppe hotel, he had suddenly remembered Ferdinand's parents and the memory had nearly ruined the honeymoon night.

Even now, some evenings before he went to bed, he hung a piece of clothing or a towel on the door handle so as to cover the lock, because, in spite of himself, he was thinking of their son.

Had Blanche noticed? Had it become a kind of signal for her?

He was a decent man, modest by nature, and also by nature he tried to be friendly with everyone.

Hadn't he succeeded in that? Certainly he had had difficult periods, particularly after he had only just left school and was working for Monsieur Depoux, the Bicêtre attorney, whose cut-stone house was only two streets away from his family's house.

Because he had successfully passed his exams, he had imagined they would give him interesting work to do, and yet they treated him like a simple office boy, indeed like an errand boy.

It was he who went to the post office, stamped the letters, put the files back on their shelves. Monsieur Depoux had a weak heart and, to avoid bringing on an attack, walked about noiselessly, almost without stirring the air around him, and talked in a low voice.

"Monsieur Jovis, you still have not remembered to empty my wastepaper basket. As for my glass of water, I despair of seeing you bring it to me at ten o'clock precisely. It is two minutes past ten."

The glass of water which helped him swallow one of the pills he took all day long . . .

"What are you thinking about, Monsieur Jovis?"

"I don't know, monsieur."

"I pay you to think of your work and not to daydream."

He had a dark corner in an office, with very poor lighting; the two clerks who worked there had no more consideration for him than the attorney.

"Run and buy me a ham sandwich, Moonface. . . ."

Luckily, it was the only time in his life when he had been given a ridiculous nickname. He had a big face, that was true enough; his skin was pale and pasty; his nose, too small for his face, looked flabby.

"You look like a moon," they had said to him two or three times at school.

In Monsieur Depoux's office he had become Moonface, and heaven knows whether it wasn't because of this that he had married a woman who could almost be called ugly.

For Blanche had an ordinary face, rather uninspiring, without any radiance, the kind one sees so often in suburban streets and at factory gates.

An orphan, she had been brought up by an aunt in Kremlin-Bicêtre, and never complained about her lot. Her aunt was a dressmaker and lived in a tiny apartment above a butcher's shop.

When she was fifteen, Blanche was taken on as an assistant, or rather a maid-of-all-work, at Peloux's grocery.

Jovis often went there to market. He had been struck by her calm, by a sort of serenity about her. Whenever someone spoke to her, she would smile, a timid smile which was enough to make her pretty.

Later he had worked at Gagnaire and Charat's, the export business on Rue du Caire; in the evening, he studied bookkeeping.

He continued these studies, as well as courses in English and Spanish, even after their marriage, when they were living on Rue des Francs-Bourgeois.

He owed nothing to fortune. He had worked hard. Blanche too, ever since her childhood.

He denied himself a third glass of white wine, tempting

though it was, for it would have been against his principles. As it was he was annoyed with himself for having had two, instead of getting along with a cup of coffee.

"Check, please."

He could leave his car where it was. It was difficult to find parking space nearer the Bastille.

He walked past the railings of the square, crossed Rue du Pas-de-la-Mule, turned left into Boulevard Beaumarchais, and looked for a moment at the pipes in a window display. For some time he had been considering giving up cigarettes and taking up a pipe, but he was afraid of looking silly.

The travel agency was situated between a restaurant and a bank. Here, too, everything had altered in the space of a few years. Monsieur Armand, Louis Barillon's son, had more advanced ideas than his father, and the front of the building and the offices had been transformed and were now bright and shining.

It was his job, with one of a bunch of keys, to raise the iron shutters and open the main door, which was made of thick glass and was electronically controlled.

The three members of the staff soon arrived, and then Mademoiselle Germaine, the stenographer, started the day, as always, by shutting herself in the washroom.

"Good morning, Monsieur Jovis."

"Good morning, Remacle."

"Good morning, Monsieur Jovis."

"Good morning, Shrimp."

Because the most recent addition to the staff, Dutoit, was only seventeen and barely five foot tall.

"Good morning, Monsieur Jovis."

"Good morning, Monsieur Clinche. . . ."

He called him monsieur because Clinche was over fifty. Actually, by seniority, it was he who should have taken over the management of the Bastille agency.

22

Monsieur Armand had been harsh with the old employee.

"I'm afraid, Clinche, that I cannot have you deal with the important customers. What are our clients coming here for? What are we selling them? Holidays! In other words, fun. And, if you don't mind my saying so, your face is rather glum."

It was true. Poor Clinche not only had a weak stomach, he even had an ulcer and, like the Bicêtre attorney, spent the whole day swallowing pills or tablets.

"You will be in charge of the back room, and you will keep in touch with the central office."

The Barillon Travel Agency was eighty years old; it had been founded by Monsieur Armand's grandfather in Boulevard Poissonnière, where the main office was still located.

In those days people didn't talk about cruise ships or airplanes, and the Barillon Travel Agency was mainly concerned with picking up luggage from private houses and forwarding it to its destination.

Nowadays there were six branches in Paris, one of them on the Champs-Elysées, which, according to Monsieur Armand, sold holidays, and, contrary to what one might have thought, the office in the far from elegant Bastille district was by no means the least busy.

A fortnight in Greece . . . Cruises in the Near East, with calls at Naples, Athens, Istanbul, Tel Aviv, Beirut . . . Spain, the Balearic Islands or, in a luxury liner, the Norwegian fjords, North Cape, and Spitzbergen.

The telephone never stopped ringing. A number of instruments were dotted about the thick glass counter, under which lay brightly colored cards.

"By bus? . . . It's possible, yes, but you'll have to change at Rome . . . Dutoit! . . . Pass me the timetable for the Rome-Brindisi buses . . . One moment . . .

23

You've got two every day, one early in the morning which arrives at . . ."

It was a question of juggling with foreign names, schedules, figures, lire, pesetas, dinars . . .

"Yes, sir . . . We have your reservation . . . If you don't mind coming this afternoon . . ."

To the left and to the right Remacle and Dutoit filled in forms and also answered telephone calls.

"What is it, Shrimp?"

"A lady asking whether the Balearic Islands are cheaper than Sardinia . . ."

"That depends . . . I'll take care of her . . . Ask her to hold on a moment . . ."

Jovis was in his element. He knew by heart the schedule of every flight, the departure dates of every ship. May had been the most hectic month, but there were still plenty of late-comers who had not yet decided where they wanted to go to.

"Have a seat, monsieur. I'll be with you in a second . . ."

On the other side of the counter there were some armchairs in real leather and two round tables, their glass tops covered with brochures.

Jovis had the use of a private office, where he saw important clients.

"Clinche, would you mind phoning Boulevard Poissonnière to find out whether there are still two cabins on the upper deck of the *Santa Clara* . . ."

Slack moments were rare. They could see people hesitating outside the window, couples discussing matters in an undertone. Generally it was the woman who led the way to the door that opened before her, and then motioned to her husband to do the talking.

"I would like to know whether the hotels in Yugoslavia are clean and whether they understand French there."

Streams of cars went past. Then, suddenly, the lights went red, the street was clear, and the pedestrians charged across.

"Yes, monsieur . . . The manager of the agency speaking . . ."

He was only thirty-five, and he was the manager. Not of the Barillon Travel Agency, of course, but of the Bastille branch. He had come a long way since his apprenticeship with Maître Depoux, who had finally died in his eighties.

"Three children under ten? . . . Personally I wouldn't advise you to go to a luxury hotel but to a family one which welcomes young people . . . You're going to the seaside, so it's better to avoid rocky coasts . . ."

He was in his element, he felt important and thought tenderly and protectively of Blanche, staying behind in their new apartment, and of Alain, who was in his last weeks at the Lycée Charlemagne.

Why worry about what the neighbors were up to?

"The manager speaking . . . I'm listening . . . I didn't recognize your voice, Monsieur Chamloup . . . Everything is arranged, yes . . . I was able to book you all in the same compartment, and you have adjacent rooms in the hotel . . . Just as you like . . . My pleasure . . ."

Chapter Two

Alain came in through the glass door just before five-thirty and went to sit down in one of the empty armchairs without greeting his father. He had evidently done his homework and prepared his lessons at the lycée, judging by the way in which he dropped his briefcase, which was always stuffed too full and had become shapeless, on the carpet beside him.

Jovis, who was still on the telephone, watched him and, as often happened, his heart skipped a beat. There was no denying it, Alain was almost beautiful. He had Jovis's broad face, but he had not inherited his ridiculous little nose, nor his prominent eyes. He had his mother's eyes, brown flecked with gold, the same gentle, seemingly peaceful look.

But the boy had his mysterious side. He observed everything about him, including his father, without giving any hint of how he was reacting, of what particularly interested him.

Emile often wondered how his son saw him, what opinion he had of him. He was happy to be seen in his real light, busy, competent, quick, un-self-conscious, knowing his business to his fingertips, switching from one language to another, friendly toward his customers but never obsequious.

He had come a long way since his apprenticeship with Depoux the attorney. For years he had sacrificed almost every evening and part of every night to his studies. The result: for the past three years he had owned a car; and for the past two days they had been living in a new and comfortable apartment.

Couldn't Alain now and then have expressed some kind of admiration? Perhaps not admiration but—how could he put it?—consideration.

Simply to take notice of his father's present position, like little Dutoit for instance, who was constantly filled with amazement.

"I wonder how you do it, Monsieur Jovis. You never seem to be pushing them. Even so, you'd be able to sell a world tour to a retired couple who were asking you for a small, inexpensive hotel on the Channel coast . . ."

Between customers, he passed near his son.

"I won't be long."

"I'm in no hurry."

Even when they were living on Rue des Francs-Bourgeois, Alain had few friends. Sometimes he could be seen walking down the street with a boy from the same school. They hardly spoke and did not look around at the girls.

"Who's your new friend?"

"He's not a friend. Just somebody from my class, Julien."

"Julien who?"

"Masereau."

"Does he live in the neighborhood?"

"In Rue de Turenne."

"Have you been to his house?"

"No."

"Do you know what his father does?"

"No."

That did not interest him. Such a question always surprised him, as if fathers didn't count, as if their jobs had no bearing on the lives of their children.

When, a little later, Jovis had closed the iron shutters of the office and they were sitting in the car, he tried to start up a conversation.

"How did it go today?"

"I don't know."

"Wasn't it hot in class?"

"The windows were open. One could hardly hear the teacher with all the noise in the street."

He hardly commented on the teachers either. His father only knew that the Latin teacher was getting old and that he blew his nose noisily.

"Do you tease him?"

"When we're bored, we blow our noses one after the other, and then all together."

"How does he react?"

"He doesn't react. He blows his nose, too. Then he says: 'Gentlemen, when you have finished, I will continue my exposition.' "

"Don't you think you make him unhappy?"

"He's used to it."

"And the other teachers?"

"They're not bad."

Was Jovis also "not bad" in his son's opinion? He could not complain about Alain. Even if he didn't study particularly hard, he still managed to get good marks and was one of the best pupils in his class. At home he was quiet, almost too quiet, reading most of the time, lying on the living-room floor or flat on his stomach on his bed.

"Why don't you go out in the fresh air?"

"Because I don't want to."

Did he have a closer relationship with his mother, when Emile was not there? He didn't dare ask his wife. The utmost he could do was ask her deceptively trivial questions.

"Does he talk to you about his school friends?"

"Very rarely."

"Don't you find him a little secretive?"

"I suppose all children are like that at a certain age."

Wasn't it Blanche's character coming out? Had he, her husband, ever really known what she was thinking deep down? She never complained even when they were hard up. At that time, before Alain was born, she used to do sewing for the neighbors, working in the evening while he studied bookkeeping and languages.

She never said she was tired. She never disagreed with his opinions.

Was one to conclude from that that she was invariably in agreement or that she was merely resigned?

They both loved one another. Whenever he thought about her, it was with tenderness, and that tenderness included a share of pity.

She had never known either her father or her mother, both of whom had been "killed in a train accident" when she was very young. That was the official story, the one which was relayed to people when they asked questions.

The truth was different, even if it did have something to do with a train. Her father, who had been a farm laborer, drank too much and ill-treated his wife. They lived in a dreary village in the north, Sainte-Marie-le-Clocher, and Raoul Chadieu had been the local terror. On Saturdays he drank more at the bar than on other days and was spoiling for a fight.

One day he and his wife had gone to Lille by train, leaving Blanche, who was only just two, with a neighbor.

On their way back, Chadieu, roaring drunk, had got in a

rage and, as they were passing some beet fields alongside the track, had pushed his wife out of the carriage door.

She died instantly.

"She jumped . . . God knows what she was thinking of . . . She's always been a bit mad . . ."

But eyewitness accounts established the fact that Chadieu had pushed her out of the train. He had managed to get away from the police. A manhunt was organized and he had held out in the woods for three days. He gave himself up in the end simply because he was starving.

Three years later, he had committed suicide in prison.

Blanche had been brought up in the suffocating atmosphere of her aunt's rooms; Joséphine Bouillet was a dressmaker, and perhaps also a little mad herself.

"Your mother must enjoy getting things settled in the new apartment."

"Sure."

Alain was hardly positive. At heart, such matters did not interest him. That morning there were still bundles of clothes and bits and pieces scattered about the rooms.

A place had to be found for each thing, life must take on a new pace, they must get used to a new light, new noises, a different setting.

"Do your school friends talk to you about what they're going to do later on?"

"Some do. Not many."

"Don't they know?"

"Some do. Those who are going into the same business as their fathers."

"And what about the others?"

"I know one who wants to become a chemist."

"And you?"

"I'll see when it's time."

Alain was vaguely watching the traffic on the throughway,

which he knew from the occasional excursion to the forest of Fontainebleau on Sundays.

Was it his age which brought out this apathy in him, or did it stem from his character, from a rooted indifference to his surroundings?

When they reached Fairview, some children were playing in the new streets and among the saplings which bent in the breeze. Airplanes passed over, soaring like arrows into a cloudless sky.

The old man with the pipe and the bloodshot eyes was in his place, in the frame of his window, like an inert object forming part of the setting. He didn't appear to see anything. Was he blind? Perhaps someone placed him there a certain number of times a day, so that he could get some air?

Nearly all the windows were open, and there were sounds of music, voices, a newscaster on the radio, an angry mother literally yelping—they caught a brief glimpse of her disheveled hair. The sound of a blow punctuated her diatribe, and the voice, suddenly calmer, concluded:

"You certainly asked for it!"

He looked at his son. He had never been hit once in his life, and yet he didn't flinch, didn't become indignant, didn't show any pity for the child.

"I like this entrance," said Jovis, walking through the double glass door, like the one in his office, except that the doors here did not open automatically.

The hall was paved with marble. There was no concierge. On one wall there were three rows of mailboxes, each with the name of a tenant and the number of the apartment. Above each there was a bell-push, and beside it a hole about an inch in diameter covered by a metal screen.

"Shall we ring?"

This amused Emile, but not Alain. He pressed the button. A little later there was a buzz, then a voice—Blanche's.

31

"I saw the car," she said. "I know it's you two."

"Did you recognize my voice?"

"Of course."

"What's for dinner?"

"Coquilles Saint-Jacques."

"We're on our way up."

A fast, smooth elevator, which did not shake like those in most Paris apartment houses. On Rue des Francs-Bourgeois, where they had lived on the third floor, there was no elevator and the stairs were dark and permanently dirty, with different smells on each landing.

He kissed his wife on the forehead, took off his jacket, and sat down at the table, while Alain carried his briefcase through the living room. The bundles had vanished from the corners of the room. The furniture had changed place noticeably and the prints were hanging on the walls.

"Is it all right that way? I didn't know where to put the one of the Battle of Austerlitz. In the end, I thought you might like to have it in our room."

He preferred not to tell her that everything would have to be changed, beginning with the furniture which they had bought piecemeal, mainly from second-hand dealers and at sales. None of it matched, it was too heavy, too dark for a modern apartment, and the prints were dotted with yellow and brown spots.

He knew he wanted to buy some Scandinavian furniture, in pale wood and with simple lines. They would talk about it later, when Blanche and Alain had had time to get used to Fairview.

"Did they come about the television?"

"Yes. It's working, and there's only a flicker on the screen when a plane flies too low."

"On Rue des Francs-Bourgeois everything blurred whenever someone in the street started his car or motor scooter."

He refused to let anyone spoil the apartment for him, and tried desperately to keep up his enthusiasm, even if it had become artificial by now.

"By the way, I met the manager's wife, Madame Lemarque."

"Did she come and see you?"

The manager lived in the house opposite, which was called Wistaria; each house was named after a flower instead of having a number. They themselves were in Primula.

"What's she like?"

"She's a nice woman, straightforward, with a head on her shoulders. I was in the self-service store when she introduced herself:

" 'You are Madame Jovis, aren't you?' "

Blanche had said yes, faltering a little, as she was a timid person and blushed easily.

"My husband has spoken about you and Monsieur Jovis. I believe you have a teen-age son at the lycée. We've got a son and a daughter, both married, so I'm a grandmother in spite of appearances."

Alain went on eating as if he wasn't listening.

"Can I have another coquille?"

"Unless your father . . ."

"No, thank you. I've had enough."

"She asked me whether I had a job. I said no. She also asked whether you came home for lunch, then she exclaimed:

" 'My dear! What are you going to do all day? With all these vacuums, washing machines, and modern gadgets, it doesn't take a woman long to do the housework. . . .' "

"What did she suggest?"

"They've put in a day nursery at Cornflower, near the turnaround. They look after children from six months to five or six years old, whose mothers work in Paris or somewhere else. . . . At the moment there are about thirty. . . . Next

33

winter they're expecting more, because all the apartments will have been sold.

"There's only one person to look after it, Madame Chartrain, the wife of a wine salesman who's nearly always away and who has no children."

"I suppose Madame Lemarque suggested . . ."

"She asked if I would agree to work for about six hours a day, three hours in the morning and three hours in the afternoon. The pay's not much, six hundred francs a month."

"What did you say?"

"That I would speak to you about it."

"What would you like to do?"

"You know I love looking after children, particularly babies."

She glanced quickly at Alain, who did not move but looked sullen. Since the age of five he had complained about having no brother or sister.

"All my school friends have got them. Why haven't I?"

Blanche and Emile couldn't very well tell him. It was not their fault that there was only the one child. After her confinement, there had been complications which had taken a turn for the worse and necessitated an operation.

The boy had often brought up the subject until about the age of ten, then he suddenly stopped. It was as if he knew.

"It's true I won't have a lot of work here. And an extra six hundred francs a month . . ."

"Let's discuss it some other time."

At eight o'clock the sun could still be seen in the west, splendidly red.

"Shall we go for a walk?" Emile suggested.

"Just as I am?"

"Of course. Just a stroll through the streets. Will you come with us, Alain?"

"No. The serial's coming on on Channel 2."

They had to get used to a new terminology. Here you didn't say streets but avenues, even though there were still neither streets nor avenues. It didn't add up to a village nor was it a town, and one could hardly talk of a development without losing face.

The air was mild and Blanche put her hand through her husband's arm. Then she withdrew it timidly.

"Why do you do that?"

"I don't know. People are watching us."

It was true. And it was a strange sensation. They were the only ones wandering slowly between the rows of new buildings.

On almost every balcony there were men and women, most of them doing nothing.

They didn't say balcony either. The word "terrace" was featured on the plans. Some already had flowers on them, predominantly geraniums in rectangular concrete window-boxes.

A few men were reading. A large woman in a flowered dress was eating sweets out of a bag which she had placed beside her on the balustrade.

The old man with the bloodshot eyes was not in his place. They must have taken him in at the same time as they took in the washing which had dried in the sun.

Impressed in spite of themselves, they spoke very little, and eventually reached the boundary. The buildings ceased. The road was no longer cemented. A large hole marked the site of a future swimming pool; there were a bulldozer and some mechanical shovels like monstrous insects lying in wait.

The path, now no more than beaten earth, crossed an undefined stretch of ground, and about a hundred yards away they could see some wheat rippling in the setting sun.

Did they both feel sad?

"Shall we go back?" she asked.

He had the impression that she had shivered. He himself did not feel at ease. He was a little lost, without anything solid around him, just as when he was a child and was sent off on an evening errand and went running through the deserted streets.

"What do you think of the idea?"

He did not understand right away.

"Oh yes—the nursery school."

"It's not a school. They've only got babies there."

"Would you like to do it?"

"I think so."

She must have made an effort to answer like that.

"Because of the six hundred francs?"

"That too. Because of everything. I think that Madame Lemarque was possibly right . . ."

He felt a pang. It was not as if it were a betrayal, of course. That would be putting it too strongly. But was it not as if Blanche were deserting their new apartment, when they had barely moved in?

It was of her especially he had been thinking when he bought it, it was she whom he imagined spending the days there. He had wanted to put her in a bright, happy setting, to provide her with the maximum comfort.

Actually, particularly since the Bastille office had been modernized, he had developed an aversion to Rue des Francs-Bourgeois, to the dark passageway and the shops exuding their strong smells, to the stairs where there was always the danger of slipping and falling, to the grimy wallpapers . . .

She glanced at him quickly.

"Do you mind?"

"No. Why should I mind? As you say, possibly Madame Lemarque is right. As the manager's wife, she must have been one of the first to come and live at Fairview."

"The very first; she told me about it. It was during the winter. They had to stop work because of the snow and the pipes were frozen. . . ."

The two women must have chatted for quite a long time. What else had they talked about? It would emerge bit by bit, over the space of a few days.

He thought about his Scandinavian furniture. Was it worth the trouble? And if he was so keen on it, if he was determined to make a clean sweep of all their old things, wasn't it for himself?

They had wandered about in a circle, and he looked at the gap between the high buildings, the pale green of the tiny trees, the façades, the shadows turning the lower part a pale gray and the setting sun tingeing the top stories pink.

"We'll see how we feel about it tomorrow."

"It's not as urgent as that. I've still got things to arrange."

She was beating a retreat, possibly because she was not sure of herself, possibly to humor him.

"What's the point of waiting?" he murmured as he lit a cigarette.

When they got back, at a quarter to nine, Alain was no longer in the living room, where the television had been switched off, nor was he in the kitchen eating something in front of the refrigerator.

Semidarkness reigned in his room, where he had gone to bed, leaving his books and notebooks piled high on the table.

He usually went to bed at nine o'clock, but he might feel tired and go and lie down whenever he felt like it. It was sometimes a kind of protest, a form of sulking.

"Everything all right, son?"

He nodded in answer.

"Good night, Alain."

"Good night."

One could never tell. Emile wanted them both to be happy. He owed it to them. He had taken over responsibility for them. Blanche and Alain depended on him. The slightest change of mood in them seemed to him a criticism, and if they were ever really unhappy he would see it as total failure on his part.

He did not know how to fill in the time before ten o'clock. He had read the paper in the morning. Blanche, on the other hand, always had things to arrange, socks to darn, buttons to sew on.

He went out onto the balcony and watched night fall, and the lamps being lit in the apartments opposite. Some tenants did not pull down the blinds and left the window open. He saw silhouettes of people whom he did not know coming and going under ceiling lights, among furniture which was foreign to him but familiar to them.

Once he saw three interiors simultaneously, on different floors. Less than three feet above the ceilings of the third-floor apartment the legs of the tenants on the fourth floor were moving about. It was like a kind of mute ballet. He could have played at guessing the words articulated by the moving lips.

A woman in a yellow dressing gown left one of the living rooms and soon came back with a crying baby in her arms.

She cradled it as she walked, while her husband went on reading an illustrated weekly. She said something to him and the husband quickly got up, took the child from her arms, and in his turn strode up and down the room singing a song, the strains of which could not be heard.

They were a young, inexperienced couple. The kitchen light went on and the wife put on some water to boil to sterilize a feeding bottle.

38

Blanche and he, too, had acted out the same pantomime, with Alain as the baby, in their apartment in Rue des Francs-Bourgeois, and Jovis wondered now whether the people opposite used to watch them.

At street level there had been a fish dealer. Opposite, he remembered, lived a policeman who used solemnly to buckle on his belt every time he went out and who wore red slippers in the evening when he was out of uniform.

On the third floor, a middle-aged woman used to wait for her daughter until midnight and often later, sitting alone before a small table covered with a plush cloth.

She began to get drowsy and one could anticipate the moment when she started to doze off and her head began to nod.

Had he tried to escape all that by coming to live at Fairview? He smoked two cigarettes in rapid succession. He smoked rarely. At the office it was forbidden, except in the small room which was his private den and where he retired now and again for a few minutes. As for little Dutoit, he went and smoked in the washroom.

"You still don't know whether you'll get a week's holiday in August?"

"That depends on the weather. If it's bad . . ."

What was the difference! Fine weather or bad weather, tens of millions of people came and went throughout the summer, and he had hardly had time to draw breath a little when he had to get down to arranging ski holidays.

Like his colleagues, he took his holidays piecemeal, during more or less dead periods, and this prevented him almost always from spending them with his wife and son.

"Alain is disappointed about going to Dieppe again."

"I know. He'd like to go to Spain, or Greece, or Yugoslavia. Unfortunately, if you were as far away as that, I couldn't join you for weekends."

39

Because of their honeymoon, they remained faithful to Dieppe and they went there nearly every year, always to the same hotel beneath the cliff.

"In two or three years' time he'll be able to travel by himself."

Blanche took fright.

"Aged fifteen! He's only just thirteen . . ."

"If you only knew the number of holidays I organize for young boys and girls of that age . . ."

Alain had barely entered high school and they were thinking already of his final exams, and after that God knows what, taking off for what destiny?

"I'm a bit tired. Shall we go to bed?"

"I'm coming right away."

He undressed, brushed his teeth, switched on the transistor radio which he kept in the bathroom so as to hear the late news. The door between the bedroom and the walk-in closet had been left open. Blanche undressed in her turn, without false modesty or coquetry, a little as if she were his sister.

She would be asleep almost the minute she was between the sheets. And he—he knew in advance—he would force himself once again to stay awake so that he could hear the noises on the other side.

"Good night, Emile."

"Good night, Blanche."

Without knowing exactly why, he hugged her to him for a moment. He felt at peace with her. She had been brave. She had not let it show that the new setting to which he had transplanted the family confused her, that she was a little frightened.

"Everything will work out all right, you'll see!"

"Yes, of course! Everything has worked out already."

She added:

"Thank you, Emile."

Thank you for what? She was like a dog which is grateful for a simple caress, and he wondered whether he did such a thing often enough.

The night before last, the goings-on in the next-door apartment had lasted barely an hour. He had seen nothing. He did not know the protagonists, they were only voices to him.

And yet it had left its mark on him. It had the same impact as the story which his friend Ferdinand had told him one morning in the elementary school playground, the one who, through the keyhole, used to watch his parents making love.

"I tell you no! It was my mother who started it," Ferdinand protested when Jovis instinctively wanted to see the woman in the role of the victim, or at least in a passive one. "She was completely naked."

Blanche's snoring, so like a hum, had begun, untroubled, regular. She was sleeping on her back, her lips half open.

The woman next door, too, had started it, but what had happened was beyond anything he could have imagined.

Sometimes, very seldom, mostly in the summer when Blanche was at Dieppe and he only joined her on weekends, when he was lying in bed in the evening he let his imagination run unchecked. He did not do it intentionally. He hardly got any pleasure out of it, indeed he tried to dismiss the erotic images which came into his mind.

Besides, it was an almost chaste eroticism. Before his marriage, he had only had a few experiences, all of them disappointing.

Basically, he could not imagine physical love without tenderness, without even a certain concern, and he had remained cold with the professional prostitutes whom he had sometimes followed to their rooms.

What had attracted him toward them was not so much desire as the heady atmosphere that surrounded them. It was mostly in the narrow streets round the Halles, near

Boulevard Sebastopol, that this went on. Usually there was a yellowish globe, giving a faint light, at the door of the hotel, and one or two women in red or green but invariably garish-colored blouses, who called out to the passers-by.

He used to walk straight on, but even so he could guess at the narrow passage, the creaking stairs, the room with its iron bedstead, its washbowl or basin.

He had gone round and round for an hour, ashamed of himself, before rushing into one of those passages, jostling the girl who was standing in the doorway almost off her feet.

"You in a hurry?"

Since his marriage, in other words during the last fifteen years, this had occurred only once.

Once also, again in August, when she had arrived at the office right after him, he had let his hand stray onto his secretary Mademoiselle Germaine's behind. She was in her forties and lived alone with her mother. Joseph Remacle, in his vulgar way, used to poke fun at her indestructible virginity and was amused to see her look of thunder.

Jovis's gesture must have surprised her, since they had worked together for years. However, she had barely given a start and had looked at him with an expression devoid of reproach—quite the contrary, Remacle would have said!

He was afraid that she would take it seriously, slip into his arms, would in the future evince something more than friendship for him.

"I beg your pardon."

Luckily, little Dutoit had come in whistling, hatless, his hair tousled as usual.

This evening he would not go to sleep, he sensed it. He felt a need to hear them again. He wanted to know more about them. He wondered if it happened every night in the same way. In the course of an hour, he had discovered a new universe, far more heady, far more dramatic than in the little streets round the Halles.

He had read novels which talk of love in crude terms and contain descriptions of improper happenings.

Reality was different.

First of all, what did those people do, the man and the woman? She had been in bed a long time before her companion came in, since Emile had not heard her go to bed. He had a key. He must be her husband or regular lover.

It was, as far as Jovis could judge, between two and three o'clock in the morning. The man made enough noise when he pushed the door open.

"Is that you?"

"Who else did you think it was?" he replied, blithely sarcastic.

"Walter might have got up."

"Walter's asleep."

"Did you go into his room?"

Who was Walter? Her husband? Her son?

"Have you been at the Carillon all this time?"

He was walking up and down and the noise of a shoe hitting the floor indicated that he was getting undressed.

"You might say so."

"You didn't go anywhere else?"

It seemed to Emile that this was not the voice of a jealous woman going over her private cross-examination. There was something else which he could not manage to define. It was true that their voices reached him only through the wall.

"You might say so . . ." the man repeated, seeming to find great satisfaction in this formula.

"Was it crowded?"

"Fairly. But no suckers today."

The word "sucker" struck him particularly. He knew its

43

meaning but, in this conversation, it was an additional mystery.

"Was Alexa there?"

"As large as life."

"Drunk?"

"Not quite passed out."

"Getting excited?"

"As usual."

"Did you go next door with her?"

"I've just come out . . ."

"From next door?"

"From her."

"Brute!"

"You asked me."

"A long time?"

"A bit shorter than last night, mercifully."

"What did she do to you?"

Each answer introduced a fresh enigma, for Jovis still could not believe that he could take the words in their usual sense. It was not possible. People do not talk like that, especially a married couple, even in a bedroom.

"Let me see if it shows. Did she bite you?"

"She can't do it any other way."

He did not say "do it." He used a more precise word, which Jovis had never uttered, which he hardly dared formulate in his mind.

"And what about you?"

"He was here."

"When?"

"At three o'clock, as usual."

"Bleating?"

"At his age, one changes only for the worse. He went on and on. I was afraid Walter would get back before he left."

"Do you think he has a suspicion?"

"You never know with him! You don't seem in a hurry."

"Give me time to recharge my batteries."

Practically every word was an insult to Jovis, to his up-bringing, to his principles. To begin with, he would have preferred not to hear. Also he was afraid that his wife would wake up and hear.

"Come here and let me . . ."

It was not possible. He refused to believe it. These people used the crudest, most graphic words and took a malicious pleasure in commenting on each one of their movements, especially the woman.

"Did she do that to you?"

"Yes."

"And that?"

"Yes."

"You bastard! I'll show you . . ."

He made an effort to visualize the scene, the characters. They must be fairly young, judging by their goings-on, but they were neither newlyweds nor lovers for the night only.

They were deeply familiar with each other, this was clear from the dialogue which came to their lips like a text learned by heart.

A text as obscene as the graffiti one blushingly reads in public washrooms.

"Wait . . . Don't move . . . It's my turn . . ."

"You're hurting me," the man objected.

"And what about her, didn't she hurt you, the bitch? If you could only stick to Irène, who's a good girl . . . Do you remember the night when it was all three of us, and I . . ."

He tried to obliterate the words he was hearing, and the images which they had evoked and which kept on coming back to him.

"No . . . Not yet . . ."

There had been other phrases, precise as the captions of

45

anatomical plates. The woman was literally beginning to rave. She was no longer a woman in the normal sense, such as one meets in the street. She was an unleashed wild animal, an animal with the gift of speech bursting into the most terrible words.

The man's Christian name was Jean. He heard that name repeated often.

"Describe it . . . Describe it . . . Tell me everything . . . what you did to her . . . what she did to you . . ."

And then he began to talk. Insatiably she pressed for further details. She went on adding:

"And that?"

"Yes . . ."

"And that . . ."

"Not so hard . . ."

"Have you suddenly become fragile?"

The pitch rose, the noises accompanying the voices became more and more defined. He waited, almost panting, for the relief which the end would provide.

"Listen . . . Put it in . . ."

In moments like that Jovis longed to hammer on the wall. His whole body shuddered with impatience, with nervousness, with indignation as well. And with fear. On no account must Blanche hear . . .

The woman cried out, in pain and pleasure, a long-drawn-out wail, and suddenly he thought he recognized the dull sound of a blow.

"Yes . . . Yes . . . Hit me again . . ."

It was not possible. It had to stop. He no longer understood.

The cry became shriller until suddenly it subsided in a kind of sob. He could have sworn that she was weeping, that she was nothing but an unhappy little girl. He almost felt pity for her.

The man must have lit a cigarette.

"You've got what you wanted, have you?" he said iron-ically but not without a touch of tenderness.

"Nearer three times than once. I thought it would never end."

"Some Scotch?"

"No water."

The clink of a bottle touching a glass, a gurgle.

"Your health, Jean."

"Yours, woman."

It was that word, uttered, at that moment, which shook Emile. Never had he himself put such complicity into his voice when he was talking to Blanche.

"Woman . . ."

It was equally true that he never called her that, that he would never think of it. Besides, she would not understand.

They had just touched rock bottom together. They had hardly emerged. With a reassuring cigarette between his lips, he poured out the drinks.

"Your health, Jean."

She sounded submissive, weary.

And he answered simply:

"Yours, woman."

That night, the third night at Fairview, Jovis waited, ashamed, straining his ears.

Chapter Three

SEVERAL times he dozed off, without really going to sleep, waking with a start when a car passed or stopped in the avenue.

Then his mind regained its lucidity, his memories of the night before last, his first night at Fairview, and, no doubt because of fatigue, his memories became distorted to the point of fantasy.

He discerned new noises in the building, distant, muffled ones, which he could not yet identify but which would eventually become integrated in his world like the familiar noises in the Rue des Francs-Bourgeois.

A car approached, a sports car to judge by the roaring of the engine and the clip with which it took the corner and stopped dead in front of the building. A door slammed. A little later, a door opened, probably the one in the next-door apartment, then, after a silence, another door, then another one, this time in the room; now he could hear the sound of steps.

A man's voice, the same as on the first night, asked:

"What are you reading?"

"A detective story."

Obviously there was some light in the room, if only the bedside lamp. He visualized the woman lying there, propped up against two or three pillows.

"You're early."

What did she call early? There was no church at Fairview, no bells, no chimes. It seemed to him that the better part of the night was over.

The man lit a cigarette, and he was probably taking off his jacket and untying his tie.

"Alexa worked fast. Admittedly, he was putty in her hands. He must have been a small-town mayor, at any rate some kind of big shot."

"Did he play ball right away?"

"It took just a couple of bottles of champagne. I was on one side of the bar, Léon was on the other."

"How much?"

"Fifteen thousand."

"A Mercedes?"

"As large as life, and twice as lovely. Little Louis had lifted it at ten o'clock on Boulevard Saint-Michel. In the time it took to go from the garage to the john . . ."

"Has he gone off?"

"Right as rain and happy as a king. Are you going to make room for me, or what?"

A silence. He got into bed. The woman asked:

"Well, anything tonight?"

"A little game with Irène."

"Does she still stare at the ceiling?"

"She couldn't. We were standing in a telephone booth."

"Do you want me?"

"Don't know yet."

Jovis was getting impatient. It was taking too long. He did not understand why it wasn't the same as on the first night, and felt almost frustrated. There was a fairly long silence. Something fell on the floor, perhaps the book which the woman had been reading.

"Are you tired?"

"No. Tonight I want to be coddled."

"You're joking!"

"Treat me as if it was the first time."

"Then there was a first time? Golly! I'd forgotten."

He heard scarcely anything more. But he thought that they were whispering in one another's ears, and that he could detect the slow, rhythmic movement of their two bodies.

"It's just as nice like that."

"Do you think so?"

"I've never met a man like you."

"Nor I a woman who can be for me all women."

"Just as well that's not true and you keep going after others!"

"With the others it's only a job."

Then they began whispering again, starting with a very soft murmur, rising to a crescendo, and ending like a child moaning.

Jovis was upset. He was angry at having had to wait such a long time, at having had to struggle with sleep and all for nothing. Now he regretted less having dropped off to sleep the night before. How could he tell that anything had happened? Perhaps the couple had gone quietly to sleep, just as he and Blanche usually did.

He tried to make sense of the snatches of conversation he had heard. There had been talk of a Mercedes, of fifteen thousand francs, of a businessman up from the country giving himself airs, who was a local mayor. A bar, with the man leaning opposite someone called Léon . . .

Blanche gave a sigh and turned over completely onto her right side without disturbing her deep sleep.

He fell asleep; at half-past six she put her hand on his shoulder and whispered:

"Time to get up, Emile."

He looked sullenly at her in her blue cotton housecoat which served as a dressing gown, then he watched the sun coming through the window as she opened the blinds.

He had drunk nothing the night before and yet his mouth felt as if it were full of sawdust.

"Didn't you sleep well?"

Attentive to the slightest variation in his expression, she noticed everything.

It was true, but he could no longer remember what he had dreamed. It had something to do with a long, shining car, like those one sees on television, moving along with statesmen standing inside, waving to the crowd. He was in the car and yet he wasn't. It was too confused, he was unable to get the images into any order.

He felt thirsty and went to pour himself a glass of water in the bathroom. Alain was in the tub, reading a detective story, and this reminded him of one episode in the night.

"Since when have you been reading those idiotic books?"

"Everyone reads them. Even politicians. Someone was talking about it in yesterday's paper . . ."

Alain must also have noticed that his father was in a bad mood, since it happened very rarely. At breakfast he hardly opened his mouth.

"Then you think I might accept?"

"Accept what?"

"The job in the day nursery."

It was too quick. She had mentioned it to him only the night before, and he had not imagined that a decision would have to be made right away.

"Do as you please."

"Do you mind?"

"No."

"But you're not happy about it?"

Alain was watching him as if he sensed something unusual in his attitude.

"Of course I am."

"I can always tell her . . ."

"Who?"

"Madame Lemarque. I can find some excuse, put it off until later."

He did not answer. He had a headache, and a dry mouth, and the coffee didn't taste right. He lit a cigarette, which tasted just as bad.

"What are you thinking about?"

"Me?"

It was absurd. He had not been drunk even once in his life. He had never had a hangover, and here he was, feeling sick inside, his brain clouded over, for no reason whatsoever.

"Let's discuss it again tonight. . . ."

He looked at her reproachfully, as this underlined the fact that she did not consider the matter settled.

"Why don't you go right ahead?"

He went down with Alain and stopped in front of the cars parked along the avenue. The vast underground garage, in construction for the Fairview tenants, would not be finished until the beginning of winter.

"I bet there'll be more than two hundred."

He gave a start. They were standing, he and his son, in front of a convertible, with a handsome red body and black leather seats.

"Whom do you think it belongs to?"

The boy raised his head and looked up at the windows in the building. Emile knew the answer, all right. It was certainly the car which he had heard draw up the night before, the one belonging to his neighbor, whose voice and vocabulary he knew but nothing else, and he preferred not to think of that at present, now that he was with his son in the bright morning sunlight.

He closed the door of his Peugeot, started it up, and drove through the no man's land where the bulldozer was at work, masking with its racket the noise of the airplanes which they could see leaving a white trail in the blue of the sky.

"It's going to be hot."

It was Alain's turn not to answer, absorbed now in his algebra book.

"I'm sorry," murmured his father, who had not noticed.

What was his neighbor's profession, if indeed he had any? He returned late at night, and this did not seem to be by choice. He wasn't a barman, since he spoke of someone called Léon who was on the other side of the bar while Alexa . . .

There wasn't only Alexa; there was also an Irène with whom he had made love in a telephone booth.

Did he sell cars? Did he buy them? Was it he who had collected the fifteen thousand francs or had he paid them out?

As for little Louis who had "lifted" the car . . .

"Watch out! You're getting into the left lane."

He blushed that a mistake of his had been noticed by his son. Half an hour later, on the terrace of the *bar-tabac* in Place des Vosges, he nearly blushed again when he ordered a glass of Pouilly. This was becoming a habit. He had always been strict with himself, had considered with something like contempt the men one sees, beginning early in the morning, drinking wine or spirits at the counter.

Today he was not drinking for the sake of drinking. It was rather to recapture the atmosphere of the day before, the mood, the excitement he had felt practically the whole day.

The wine was new, the glass misty, the waiter indifferent. He opened his paper.

They had mentioned the Carillon, which could be the name of a café, or a restaurant or night club. More likely a night club, since the man returned from it in the middle of the night.

He got up and walked toward the telephone booth, not without thoughts of the girl they had called Irène, who appeared to be uncomplicated. In the telephone directory he found one Carillon, in Boulevard Saint-Martin, but that was a watchmaker's shop. There was even a Monsieur Carillon, Henri, a chartered accountant who lived on Rue Caulaincourt. There was also a Mademoiselle Carillon, Hortense, no profession given.

At last, the Carillon Doré, a night club on Rue de Ponthieu. It was only twenty minutes past eight. There was plenty of time for him to go and have a look at it, but he would have considered that too ridiculous.

What was he poking his nose into? His neighbors were none of his business. He wouldn't even have known them on the street.

And here he was getting mixed up in their private life!

"Waiter! The same again . . ."

He crossed and uncrossed his legs, took the paper from the chair beside his, then put it back.

"Check, please."

He didn't want to read. It was a long time since he had been in the neighborhood of the Champs-Elysées. He went around by the left bank, drove along the quays, crossed the Pont de la Concorde. All the cars, at this hour, were streaming toward Paris and forming a herd which the white batons of the police and the red traffic lights cut into sections.

As he drove up the Champs-Elysées, he noticed the Barillon agency, with its glass window. Inside were a vast white marble room, travel posters and shining desks, chairs waiting for the employees, green armchairs for the customers.

54

The even vaster office in the rear, with its three or four telephones, belonged to Monsieur Armand, the younger Barillon.

As for old Barillon, who was eighty-two, he retained his room in the company's head office, on Boulevard Poissonnière, where nothing had changed for the last sixty years, if not longer.

Emile's curiosity about his neighbors seemed to him increasingly ridiculous. The Barillons, their agencies, Monsieur Louis, Monsieur Armand, and their ancestor, Monsieur François, with his side whiskers and frock coat, known to the employees only from a photograph, represented duty, peace of mind and spirit, and also Jovis's success, since he had become, by dint of application, one of the important wheels in this business.

He had gone almost all around the Arc de Triomphe and turned in the direction of the Bastille, but he nevertheless entered Rue de Ponthieu, where the waiters were tidying up the cafés and bars.

Most of the shops were still closed. Above a pale-blue façade, which made him think of a dairy, he read the words: LE CARILLON DORÉ, and a wooden bell, painted gold, was hanging above the door.

Pleated curtains concealed the interior. To the right of the door, in a frame fixed to the wall, there were photographs of women in various stages of undress.

"Striptease."

There were fifty night clubs of the same sort in the neighborhood, and Jovis had never pushed open the door of one of them. He was disappointed. It seemed to him that the mystery was evaporating, that the story was becoming humdrum, vulgar.

Alexa, whose amorous technique had been detailed by his neighbor, undressed ten times every evening in front

55

of the customers. So must Irène, the gentle, passive girl. Others as well, no doubt.

As for the man . . .

Was he the proprietor of the establishment? And was the woman, for her part, a retired striptease artist?

He pushed down sharply on the accelerator because a car just behind him was warning him by a light sound of its horn that he was holding up the traffic.

He had an appointment at half-past nine with a lawyer who wanted to organize a safari for about ten of his friends. It was a big thing.

Finally he found a place to park his car, and a few minutes later he went through the ritual, almost sacred gesture of raising the iron shutter.

Mademoiselle Germaine was just behind him, in an orange dress with sweat stains under the arms. There were also beads of sweat on her upper lip, and he noticed for the first time some down on it.

"It's going to be hot."

"Yes."

"It's next week, isn't it, you begin your vacation?"

"On Monday."

"Where are you going?"

"To the mountains, in Savoy. My mother loathes beaches."

"And what about you?"

"She's old. I've got to adjust to her."

She was forty. With her mother she was still an obedient little girl. It was the same with him, with his father. . . .

On Sunday, three days from now, he would go and see him at Kremlin-Bicêtre. Alain, as usual, would be in a bad mood. However, they went only every other Sunday, in the afternoon, because his father lived alone and did not want to cook for the whole family.

As he thought of it Emile had the impression of touching ground again in reality. While waiting behind the counter for his first customer, he prepared the safari file, automatically nodding to the three employees who arrived at almost the same time.

"Monsieur Clinche, would you come here a minute? Didn't we get a letter recently from Bill Hatworn, our Kenya correspondent?"

"It's already been filed. I'll get it for you."

So, all the same, the day was off to quite a good start. The lawyer did not arrive until ten. He was a small, fat man, chubby and pink-faced, and it was hard to imagine him, in safari clothes, lying in wait for a lion or a leopard. Nevertheless, this would be his third safari, and he had converted many of his friends to the idea.

They sat down in armchairs and discussed flight schedules, hotel prices, panoramic views of Kenya, the Sudan and the Congo.

At noon, Jovis sat down alone at the far end of the little restaurant he had discovered close by in Rue Jacques-Coeur, where the menu was written up in chalk on a slate and where, through the door which was always open, the owner's wife could be seen bending over her stove.

"Unfortunately, calf's head doesn't agree with me."

"We can fix you a cutlet."

On the wall there were racks containing the regulars' napkins, and it would not be long before his was there. Alain would be having lunch at school. Joseph Remacle, who lived on Boulevard Voltaire, would go home for lunch, while little Dutoit ate in a snack bar, like Mademoiselle Germaine.

Only Monsieur Clinche was left at the office, with all the doors locked. Either for reasons of thrift or from habit he brought his meal wrapped in black oilcloth, and if the telephone rang he did not answer it, as he was off-duty.

57

Did it all have to do with a gang of car thieves? He was thinking about it against his will. He read the papers like everyone else, and knew that dozens of cars were stolen every day and only half or two thirds of that number were ever recovered.

The rest, repainted, were driven over one of the borders to be resold abroad.

He had never been in a position to see a thief at close quarters. He had discovered only three years previously that one of the employees, who had of course been dismissed immediately although Monsieur Armand had decided not to prosecute, had not been entering certain incoming sums of money and in this way netted for himself several hundred francs a month.

He was an older man, about fifty, as gloomy as Monsieur Clinche, married, with two children, one of whom was at medical school.

He had burst into tears. It was pathetic.

"How long have you been at it?"

"Less than six months. I expected to be able to repay it. I was sure. Luck can't always go against me."

"What did you do with the money?"

He didn't run after women, he wasn't an extravagant spender. What he earned went to pay for his sons' education and he lunched on sandwiches in a brasserie on Faubourg Saint-Antoine.

"Cards . . ."

Jovis had looked at him with amazement. Was he so naïve, at his age, as to be astonished at a man so addicted to gambling that he would embezzle the petty cash?

It was not only pathetic, it was disillusioning.

"I beg you, Monsieur Jovis, give me a chance. I swear it'll never happen again. You can keep back part of my salary every month. If my sons . . ."

It was strange. Jovis would have been quite uncompromising, as he had a strict notion of honesty.

Monsieur Armand, who came to the office the following day because of the incident, was a big, strong man, dressed with care, close-shaven, exuding a faint smell of apéritifs and liqueurs.

He had remained standing while the culprit was talking. "What do you think, Jovis?"

"It's up to you to decide, Monsieur Armand. He admits to having juggled the books and cheated us for more than six months."

"He's been with the firm for fifteen years, hasn't he?"

"Sixteen."

"He was here before you, then?"

"I was hired three years later and started work at the Boulevard Poissonnière office."

"I know. Well, settle what we owe him and give him a certificate simply saying that he has worked here for such and such a time, without any comment."

The thief began to cry again, this time for joy, and if they had not stopped him he would have kissed Monsieur Armand's hand.

It was strange. It was an unjust decision. Jovis, who had worked so hard, who had never cheated anyone of so much as a centime, had waited five years before asking timidly for a raise.

Was his neighbor also a thief?

A happy thief, without a bad conscience, lusting for life and caring only about making love.

All three of them dined together, the living-room windows wide open, while the news was being broadcast on television. Only Alain listened fitfully. Emile watched his wife, who was sitting opposite him, as if he were seeking in her face something new and different, or even as if he were wondering why it was she and not someone else he had chosen for his wife.

He was very young when he had met her, not quite twenty. Her humility, her patience, her lack of resentment against fate or against mankind had touched him. When he asked her out one Sunday afternoon, he did not know that he would make his decision the very same evening. She did not suspect it either. He brought the matter up only three weeks later.

"Did you go to the nursery?"

"The day nursery. Madame Lemarque is quite insistent on calling it that."

"Did she go with you?"

"She came to fetch me. She's not a woman who will take no for an answer. Not only did I go along, but I stayed there."

"What do you mean?"

"Up to five o'clock I did the work which I'll be doing every day from tomorrow morning."

"Do you enjoy it?"

"That's not the right word. I love children. There are about thirty in a bright room on the ground floor at Cornflower. There's another room for the babies, a kitchen, washrooms. A french door opens out onto a lawn surrounded by white railings, and the children play there under an awning. There's even a little swimming pool made of some kind of plastic which can be inflated and filled with water."

"What are the hours?"

"From nine in the morning until three in the afternoon. I'll have lunch with the children, so I won't have to cook just for one person."

One never knew with her whether she was really happy or not, as she would shrink from mentioning any of her troubles or difficulties.

"Madame Chartrain, the other woman, who's been there for three months, is very sweet and kind, and the children adore her. She does everything they want. In the beginning they pushed her out on the grass and three or four of them jumped up and down on her."

He smiled at the idea of Blanche in the same position. Wouldn't she feel awkward, self-conscious?

"I can't even hear the commentator speak," Alain protested.

They were silent. The commentator's voice was the only one reverberating in the room, and it was echoed by the same voice in another apartment where the windows were also open.

"Have you got any work to do, Alain?"

"No. Why?"

"We might go out for a bit."

"In the car?"

"For a walk."

He made a face, as he didn't like walking, in spite of all his talk about sports and knowing all the names of the champions.

"What about you, Blanche?"

"I have still got to mend Alain's trousers and iron them."

Jovis felt like strolling in the setting sun, as on the evening before, and he was about to resign himself to going out alone when his son relented.

"Okay! Wait for me. I'm coming. . . ."

They walked down the four flights of stairs as if to familiarize themselves with the smells of the building. On Rue des Francs-Bourgeois, they changed with every floor, almost with every step. Here the only smell was of still fresh masonry and of paint. Their steps echoed on the tiles in the entrance hall, and it did not occur to Jovis to consult the cards over the mailboxes, to discover his neighbor's name.

61

"The red car isn't back," Alain remarked, examining the line of cars. "I'm not surprised."

"Why?"

"Because someone with a car like that doesn't get home early."

His father looked at him with surprise, struck with this deduction. At the same instant, Alain raised his head and fixed his eyes on a point in space. He did the same, and realized what had interested his son.

Two windows away from theirs, on the same floor, a boy of fourteen or fifteen was leaning out and looking down. The two boys might have been conducting a mutual examination.

The one at the window seemed rather fat, with rounded shoulders and a thick neck. He had the look of an astonishingly placid dummy.

His face impressed Jovis by its calmness, the depth of the brown eyes, the whiteness of the skin, the black of the long hair, which was slightly curly.

It lasted only for a few seconds. Alain had shown no surprise, and he was the first to move on.

"Do you know him?"

"I've heard him."

"What did you hear?"

"He's our neighbors' son. His room is next to mine. He's got a marvelous hi-fi, which must have cost at least two thousand francs."

Alain had only a standard turntable and about twenty records at the most which he had bought with his pocket money.

"He's got all the best English and American jazz groups."

"Have you spoken to him?"

"It's the first time I've seen him."

Why did everything concerning his neighbors have such a fascination for Jovis? Lots of children are plump at that boy's age and look like dummies. One often sees dummies with black hair, dark eyes, and colorless skin.

Yet, in spite of himself, he was surrounding this child with a halo of mystery.

"Where are we going?"

"Nowhere. Just for a walk."

Actually he knew where he wanted to go, and drew his son toward the end of the avenue, toward the future swimming pool and its bulldozer, then along the dirt road.

There, where the paving began again, there were wheatfields on the left, a grove on the right, and twice already he had nearly got out of his car as he drove past.

Alain looked at this scenery with indifference; all he did was break off the end of a branch and whip it through the air. Emile, though, was watching out for the cornflowers and poppies among the spikes of wheat. He broke off an ear, touched the grains, still warm from the sun of the day, and, removing the husks with his teeth, started to eat them.

"You like that?"

"It reminds me of my childhood."

"Is that a good thing?"

Alain did not understand. For Jovis, it was the walks on Sunday along the Seine which were conjured up, his father in a straw hat, his mother, whose image he found difficulty in evoking but whom he always imagined in a blue dress.

There was invariably a moment when they sat down on the grass and sometimes it was beside a wheatfield dotted with blue and red.

"Shall we sit down for a moment?"

"Do you really want to?"

Emile did not dare insist. His own father, after the picnic, used to stretch himself out and doze off, with a newspaper over his face and the flies buzzing around him.

The river water had a special smell, compounded of damp

earth or mud, with a fishy aroma, as they used to find on the bank fish which were too small and had been left by the anglers.

"It's funny to see the country begin so abruptly," Alain remarked, turning toward the tall white buildings which stood barely four hundred yards away.

A pity that he wouldn't sit down. To tell the truth, Jovis had come on purpose to wallow in memories, in innocence. He breathed in deeply, seeking to rediscover the spells of long ago.

"What do you think—shall we go back?"

"If you like."

There was melancholy in the air, in spite of the very clear sky, brushed with a water-color pink as on the evening before, streaked with long white trails which did not evaporate until long after the airplanes had gone over.

"Do you expect to become friends?"

"With whom?"

"With the boy you saw at the window."

"I don't want him hanging around my neck. But I'd like to hear his records."

"You hear them from your room."

"It's not the same thing."

"Have you seen his mother and father?"

"No."

Alain looked at him, surprised by these questions, commonplace enough but unexpected.

"Yesterday you were complaining about having to find new friends."

"That's no reason to take up with just anyone."

If they had sat down on the grass, perhaps Emile would have stretched out, if only for a moment.

Had he had more sustained conversations with his father? He didn't remember any. Even now, when he went to see him every other week, the replies were disjointed, interrupted by silences.

However, the background was familiar. Nothing had changed in the house, not even his mother's iron, which was still in the same cupboard.

The old teacher preferred to do his own cooking after going for an apéritif to the café at the corner where he found three or four men of his own age. From the terrace he could see in the distance children kicking up the dust as they came out of the school where he had taught for so many years.

Alain didn't like the old-fashioned little house at Kremlin-Bicêtre. Those visits to his grandfather were for him a distasteful constraint to which he complied only with a show of temper.

He did not understand how one could sit in a tiny room, or in a patch of garden surrounded by walls, doing nothing, staring into space, letting time slip by, occasionally uttering a sentence with no relevance whatsoever.

When he was a child, Emile did not have to go and visit his grandfather and grandmother, who lived in the center of France and were dead by the time he was old enough to travel.

He still felt vaguely ill at ease before the enlarged photographs prominently displayed in the dining room of the little house.

"What are you thinking about, Alain?"

"Nothing. I don't know."

"Are you still sorry we've moved?"

"That depends."

"On what?"

"On all sorts of things."

"When you get back from your holiday, I'll buy you a motor scooter."

"I won't have to wait until Christmas?"

"No."

Emile was not proud of himself. He seemed to be buying his son's complicity. But complicity in what?

It was a little as if he had an inkling of a new secret link between them. By force of circumstances, and in spite of his resistance, Alain would end up by meeting the boy they had seen at the window.

Jovis, for his part, one day would see the woman and the man whom he knew only by their voices—voices, it is true, which laid bare to him their most secret life.

It frightened him a little. He caught sight of another world that was unknown, dangerous. As a good father, shouldn't he have said to his son: "Watch out, Alain. He's not the right friend for you"?

Because of what? Because of the words, the gasps, the moans, the obscenities which he had heard, which he had waited for on the other side of the wall, because of the gestures, the images which he strove to conjure up?

There was peace and quiet all around them. It was not like Rue des Francs-Bourgeois, there were no pedestrians on the sidewalks, no old men sitting on their front-door steps, no shops open late. There was no movie house in the neighborhood.

Everyone was in his own pigeonhole, with a record playing, the radio, television, or a child whining because it was being put to bed.

Now and then an engine started and a car drove toward the throughway. As they passed in front of the houses, they heard voices, scraps of isolated sentences which made no sense.

They took the elevator on the way to their apartment. Blanche was busy ironing in semidarkness.

He remembered a picture he had seen, a woman in a pale

blue apron, her hair caught in a knot, ironing in just the same way in the half-light. It was a pointillist work and the minuscule spots, in pale colors, surrounded the central figure with a faintly luminous blur.

He didn't remember the painter's name. It didn't matter.

"Good night, Ma."

"Are you going to bed already?"

"I think he's going to listen to the music instead."

"What music?" asked Blanche in astonishment.

Alain gave his father an angry look as if to reproach him for breaking a confidence.

Emile had been wrong. He had spoken without thinking. His mind was too much on those people who lived on the other side of a thin wall and who had nothing to do with his family's existence or with himself.

It was just because he was angry with himself that he had, almost treacherously, put Alain in a difficult spot.

"Good night, son. I was joking. I was thinking of all the music one hears in this building."

His wife looked at him. When three people live intimately, each one becomes sensitive to mere nothings, to an inflection, an unusual word, to a gesture, to a look.

When Alain had left the room she asked:

"Did you go far?"

"As far as the wheatfield."

"Which wheatfield?"

"At the end of the building site."

He had said "building site" for want of a better word.

"A little farther on from what will be the swimming pool. Let's go there again on Sunday."

"It's one of your father's Sundays."

"I'll ring him and say we haven't finished moving in. To make up for it I'll pick him up next Sunday and bring him over for lunch. I want him to get to know our new place."

"I must buy some trousers for Alain. I don't know how he manages to tear them so quickly."

Why did he feel the need to go to his son's room? Alain was in bed, with the light turned off.

"Is that you, Daddy?"

"I forgot to kiss you good night."

He could hear the music, in the next-door room, music he didn't know, muffled and haunting, split now and then by a piercing scream, and he thought of the woman whom he had heard crying out in the middle of the night.

"Who's playing?"

"A new group from San Francisco. A boy at school told me about it. He's got the record. But it's a stereo that costs twenty-eight francs."

"Would you like to buy it?"

"With what?"

"Suppose I offered to give it to you?"

"Why?"

They were not a family which made a habit of giving presents except for a particular occasion.

"Let's say it's to celebrate our move."

"If you want to . . ."

He added after a silence:

"Thank you."

He was eager to be alone again and to listen to the music.

While Blanche was undressing with her usual modesty, Emile wanted very much to make love to a woman. He hesitated. He knew it was not she whom he desired but a woman, any woman except her, a woman who . . .

He was angry with himself for having drawn Blanche, even for a second, into his troubled thoughts. She lay down beside him, he felt the warmth of her body, and when he kissed her there was a little dampness around her lips.

68

"Did you leave the window open on purpose?" she asked.

He replied without thinking:

"The heat's oppressive. If there's a storm, I'll go and close it."

For even a storm did not waken his wife.

"Good night, Emile."

"Good night, Blanche."

Was the other woman already in bed, on the other side of the wall? Was she busy reading her detective story by the light of the bedside lamp, a light which, for no reason, he thought of as pink?

He imagined also a room markedly different from theirs, a low bed, very wide, with a satin cover, an easy chair, fragile furniture with silky reflections in the wood. He would have wagered that the telephone was white and that there was wall-to-wall carpeting in a light color.

This time he did not consciously try to keep awake. It was not deliberate that his imagination was wandering.

Was she dark like the boy they had seen at the window, or was it the man who had somewhat oriental features?

Was she also obese?

These images did not fit in with their voices. The man's, always a trifle sardonic, had nothing mellow about it. It was a voice one associated more with giving orders than with dreaming.

"Walter!"

It was she, very close to the wall, so she must be in bed. She called twice, three times, her voice getting progressively louder, but the boy did not hear from his room, because of the music.

Emile "sensed" her feeling about for her slippers with the toes of her bare feet, moving away, going to speak to her son—because it could only be her son—and the music suddenly stopped.

She was gone for a long time and it was the noise of the door, then that of the mattress, which told him that she had got back into bed again.

On one side, Jovis had his wife, already asleep, with her thigh pressed against him; he had his son, his furniture, his home, the humble little human cell which he had laboriously built up.

On the other, behind the wall, a woman whom he had never seen, a woman who would be joined again by a man in the middle of the night and whose searing voice he would perhaps hear.

He felt himself being torn in two directions, guilty already even though he had done nothing.

Although his father was an atheist, Emile had been baptized and had learned his catechism. Since then, he had been in a church only when he had got married or been to a funeral service.

Even so, scraps from religious texts still inhabited his memory and he now had the impression of being a Christian on the verge of losing his faith.

He needed to sleep.

Chapter Four

IT was a Sunday without bells, without old women in black going to Mass from six o'clock onwards, without families in their Sunday best walking along the streets.

On the other hand, there were more sounds of car engines, more bursts of conversation. People were piling into cars. One mother was calling out of the window on another floor to ask whether they had remembered to take their swimming suits or the thermos. The children were quarreling about who should sit by the doors, and already blows were being exchanged.

Most of them were off to the sea, a certain number to the woods, and some, no doubt, were driving without any destination, straight ahead of them.

Emile Jovis slept late, conscious of this agitation going on in the apartment house, and he found Blanche hovering in the living room, where the french windows onto the terrace were wide open.

He kissed her on the cheek. They seldom kissed on the mouth. That, for them, was the prelude to sexual relations, and it would have seemed indecent, for example, to kiss like that in Alain's presence.

"Did you sleep well?" she asked him.

He answered in the affirmative, which wasn't true. He had tried. But there had been the voices, the litany of foul language, of obscene phrases.

This time he had tried not to listen. He had just managed to get to sleep again when a groan or a cry woke him with a start. The action seemed to him to go on forever. Finally it turned into a nightmare. Would they never tire of this comedy next door? Because, to him, it seemed unthinkable that two normal human beings . . .

He even wondered whether they were not aware of his presence on the other side of the wall and were amusing themselves by mystifying him, winking at one another every now and then.

He could have sworn that, the last time he opened his eyes, a little daylight was filtering through the shutters and almost immediately afterwards the cars were driving along the avenue and the other nearby streets.

He drank his coffee, standing in the kitchen. There were no croissants. The baker didn't come on Sundays. Besides, they didn't have them every day. It depended on how they felt.

It was after eight o'clock, and he thought of the sunny terrace on Place des Vosges, of the misty cold glass, of the joyful color of the Pouilly.

"Is Alain still asleep?"

"Isn't he in the bathroom?"

So he was the first to use the bath, and he stayed there in a dream longer than usual. Then he shaved while he listened to the news on the radio. Accidents on the highway already, of course. Statistics. So many cars per hour going west and so many going south. Fine weather at Deauville and a bottleneck at Auxerre.

Deep down he loved to spin out his Sunday morning in this way, even if he felt tired or peevish. He put on his trousers and an open-neck shirt, and went out onto the terrace to watch the comings and goings of the development.

More than half the cars had gone already, leaving large gaps between the ones still there. The red sports car was right below him. He looked toward the Farrans' apartment. For now he knew his neighbors' name. Jean Farran. The card on the mailbox belonging to their apartment gave no indication of his profession.

There were all sorts of people in the building, people of independent means and young households, many families and a Mademoiselle Marcouli, a spinster. French names and foreign names. A Zigli, a family called Diacre, and various Descubes, Delaos, Pipoirets, and Lukaseks.

Those who gave some indication of their profession included an appraiser, an engineer, a manicurist, and a head clerk at the finance ministry.

It was certainly too early for Farran to come out on the terrace. He must be asleep, and Jovis imagined them both, the man and the woman, without even a sheet over them because of the heat.

"Are you cooking me some eggs, Ma?"

Alain, still in his pajamas, looked blurred with sleep. He didn't say good morning but held up his forehead, first of all to his mother, then to his father, before sitting down at the kitchen table.

"How do you want them?"

"Boiled. No, fried. Don't forget to turn them."

"Did you sleep well, son?"

A grunt. He was slow getting going, and tried to drink his coffee when it was too hot.

"What are we going to do today?"

And, hostile as ever:

"Are we going to Kremlin?"

"No. I telephoned my father to say we'd skip a visit."

"Are we going to go out for lunch?"

"I think we'll stay here. It's our first Sunday at Fairview. Your mother still hasn't had time for a real walk around here."

"When are you going to buy me the scooter?"

"Tomorrow, if you like."

"Will there be a shop open at six o'clock?"

"There are always some open on Avenue de la Grande-Armée."

"May I use it to go to Paris?"

"Not the first few times. You'll have to get used to it!"

"It's no harder than a bike, and I had a bike when I was eight."

Emile helped his wife move the sideboard in the dining-room part of the living room. Their furniture was particularly heavy and sturdy.

"We'll buy other pieces. I've seen some sets of Swedish furniture in a pale wood, I don't know which, probably ash."

"Do you think we can afford the expense?"

Was it really the expense she was thinking about? She had not protested when he had talked of buying an apartment at Fairview and she had docilely allowed herself to be trans-planted from Paris.

If Alain was losing his friends, she was losing the familiar shops, her daily routine, the women she met and with whom she chatted.

And now they were going to change the furniture as well!

"Don't forget that from now on you too will be making money."

"Provided I please them."

"How did it go yesterday?"

"Quite well. It's a strange feeling to be surrounded by so many children all at the same time. At first, you panic. Madame Lemarque comes along from time to time to see that everything is going all right. As for Madame Chartrain, she never gets nervous. You would think she didn't realize her responsibilities. She's a sad woman. I wonder if it's really because of his job that her husband is nearly always away. Madame Lemarque hinted at an affair.

" 'Try to get her mind on something else,' she told me.

"Because Madame Lemarque is interested in everything, she knows what goes on in each apartment."

Alain had slipped on an old pair of beige trousers and a polo shirt. His feet were bare in his sandals. It was his way of marking Sunday.

"Are you going out?"

"I don't know."

He dropped into an armchair and flipped through a magazine while his father, just as confused as he by this first Sunday in an unknown world, went out again onto the terrace.

He drew back at once. There was someone on the terrace to the right, a tall, fair man, with nothing on but a light-colored pair of shorts.

His bare chest, thick and muscled, was tanned by the sun.

He lit his cigarette with a lighter which from a distance looked like gold, and as he raised his head Jovis drew back a little farther, as if he were afraid of being noticed by his neighbor.

It was probably Jean Farran. They were about the same age, most likely, but the other man was more vigorous, more strapping, and there was an assurance in his stance which Jovis had never known except when he was juggling with timetables and itineraries in his office.

He was talking, turning toward the interior of his apartment, asking, like Jovis a little earlier with his son:

"Are you going out?"

Was he talking to the boy or to his wife? Emile couldn't hear the reply. Farran flicked the ash from his cigarette over the balustrade, and then leaned against it. His back was as muscled as that of a physical training instructor, and he had the profile of a man who has no doubts about himself.

Without admitting it, Emile was jealous of him. It wasn't fair. He did not try to specify what was not fair, but after those agitated nights it was not the image he had formed of his neighbor.

"Do you need me, Emile? Can I go and have my bath?"

After fifteen years of marriage, she still locked the bathroom door.

The man finished his cigarette, sent it flying into space with the flick of a finger, and watched it go for a moment before stepping back into his apartment.

A few moments later, Jovis saw the boy with the black hair and the dark eyes on the sidewalk. He too was wearing shorts, but with a short-sleeved yellow shirt. He stood there, undecided, looking about him as if for something to do, then he walked slowly to the left.

Emile felt someone beside him. It was his son, who, like him, was watching their young neighbor walking away up the deserted avenue. There was a short silence.

"I'm going for a walk."

And Alain was already gone, as usual banging the apartment door. His father jumped every time it happened. He did not know how to take this brutal gesture which he thought of as a form of aggression. He didn't dare say anything, remembering his father, who, when he was a boy, came out onto the doorstep and called him back.

"What is it?"

"Nothing. Come back a moment. Good! Now, you'll go out and close the door like a civilized human being."

Gritting his teeth, Emile used to obey, but over the years he had grown angry with his father.

"You must get used to behaving toward other people as you would want them to behave toward you."

The same thing at meals. Nothing escaped his teacher's eye.

"Your elbow!"

"I'm sorry."

Or else it was the tablecloth on which he was drawing with the prongs of his fork. Or his head was too low over his plate.

Did he love his father? He respected him, certainly. In a way he admired him, especially when he in his turn had a son. But he had never felt really close to him. Yet they had lived alone together for years in the little house, with only a cleaning woman coming in two hours a day and, on Saturday, the whole day for a thorough cleaning.

His father judged and did not allow himself to be judged. Feeling himself observed calmly, lucidly, without indulgence, Emile used to be seized with panic and would have been capable of every kind of rebelliousness.

However, he had not rebelled. He had learned to close doors noiselessly and to sit up straight at table. He had also learned to do his best, even at the least important things, and it was because of this that he had become what he was.

A few days earlier, he was proud of this fact. He had risen as high as possible, given his point of departure in the social scale.

One day old Monsieur Louis would die. His son, Monsieur Armand, would almost certainly proceed without delay to modernize the head office on Boulevard Poissonnière, and install himself there.

And then it would be Emile's turn, in view of his success at the Place de la Bastille office, to take over as head of the Champs-Elysées agency.

That constituted his ceiling. Impossible to go higher, because there was a young Barillon who, after studying law, had come into the business and would succeed his father in his turn. Actually there were two brothers Barillon, but Monsieur Jacques was crazy about cars and women, and gave more cause for worry than for hope.

Now Alain was walking alone along the sidewalk, in the direction which their young neighbor had taken. Alain was taller. He wasn't fat. If he were a bit more athletic . . .

Jovis heard a murmur of voices beside him. It came to him, not through the wall as at night, but through the open windows on the calm, warm air of a Sunday.

He could not make out the words. It sounded like a peaceful, desultory conversation and once, when the woman appeared on the balcony, Jovis had to step back another time.

She was wearing a silk dressing gown printed with small multicolored flowers, and elegant gold slippers. She had her back turned toward him and he could not see her face, only her dark hair, which hung down a good four inches below the nape of her neck.

"I thought I saw Walter . . ."

She was smoking. Her nails were long and red. She was going back in already, talking as she went. Other men, other women, in the houses opposite, were coming and going in the same way, some to a background of music, some, alone, in a strange silence.

Was the old man with the red-rimmed eyes sitting at his window? Whom did he live with? Someone must look after him, because he gave the impression of an invalid who was installed in his place at a fixed hour, and taken inside again to be fed like a child.

That might happen to his father one day. He was still alert and capable of taking care of himself. But ten years, twenty years from now?

"Are you bored?"

It was Blanche's voice, in the living room. She was wearing the blue housecoat which she only took off to go out.

"I'm watching people."

"Don't you think they're very different from the ones in Rue des Francs-Bourgeois?"

"On the average they're younger."

He recalled the passers-by, in the narrow street in the old quarter, and suddenly realized that the majority they saw there were old people, particularly old women.

"Did Alain tell you where he was going?"

"For a walk."

"He seems a bit lost. I wonder whether he'll get used to it."

"It won't be long before he finds some friends."

There was a silence. Blanche was rearranging the few flowers which remained from a bunch her husband had given her to celebrate their arrival in the apartment.

"Perhaps I'm mistaken," she said in that even voice which never expressed passion or drama, "but it seems to me that people here strike up friendships less easily. Each one lives his own life."

Just because he too had thought he sensed this, from the very first day, he felt obliged to protest.

"Don't forget that we've barely moved in, that lots of people don't even know us by sight."

"There are no shops, except for the self-service one, where I wouldn't think of talking to people."

"Madame Lemarque talked to you."

"Because she wanted me to do something."

"Do you feel discouraged?"

"No."

She in turn came out onto the balcony.

"Look! There's Alain coming back. He's got someone with him."

She was smiling her unobtrusive smile.

"You're right. He hasn't taken long to find someone to talk to."

They were walking back together, he and Walter, exchanging words and sometimes gestures whose significance could not be understood from such a distance.

Alain was the taller one. And it was he who spoke most frequently, and with considerable animation.

The other boy listened calmly, almost placidly, nodding his head, occasionally contributing a few words. His lips, in contrast with his pale complexion, seemed very red, like those of a woman.

Emile quickly stepped back into the living room, as the woman next door came out again onto her balcony. Why did he feel it necessary to hide from them? It was as if he were afraid of being recognized, as if they had been able to see him during the night when he was listening to them on the other side of the wall.

He would certainly have blushed if they had seen him, especially the woman, whom he seemed to know so intimately. If someone had introduced him to her, he would probably have remained speechless, seized with a longing to run away.

"They're both coming back into the house."

He knew, but he did not tell Blanche that he knew. He did not want to talk to her about their neighbors, and he was terrified at the idea that their son was about to do this very thing.

"What do we have for lunch?"

"Lamb chops and green beans."

"With mashed potatoes, I bet."

Alain didn't like mashed potatoes on Sundays.

"No, with baked potatoes. That reminds me, it's time to get the vegetables started."

Alain did not mention his new acquaintance.

"Does he live in this block?" asked his mother.

"Who? Walter?"

"His name's Walter? Walter who?"

"I didn't ask him."

"Is he French?"

"I imagine so. In any case, he speaks French as well as I do. Why do you ask me that?"

"I only saw him from up here, but I thought he looked foreign."

"At school there are some boys who've got just as black hair as he."

"Is he nice?"

"He buys all the records he wants. He's invited me to go and listen to them whenever I feel like it."

"Are you going?"

"Why shouldn't I?"

"He didn't tell you what his father does?"

"That doesn't interest me."

It was a question which Emile, too, had often asked him. Alain went out with his friends, went to their homes, sometimes had meals with them, and he would have liked to know what their background was.

"What's his father's business?"

His son always stiffened, giving the question a twist that it did not have. He probably attributed it to a kind of snobbery in his father, or to a desire to see him mix only with "better-class" people.

Were they in the process of interrogating Walter in the next-door apartment?

"What time did you ask him for?"

"Whenever he wants to come. He likes the same music as I do, but he hasn't got any records."

"Did he tell you what his father does?"

Alain went off to his room, Blanche to the kitchen, and Emile dropped into an armchair and reached for a magazine.

He was happy. . . . His father was happy. . . . His wife was happy. . . . What about Alain?

He must be too. He had every reason to be. . . .

"If one has any sense of responsibility . . ."

And also:

"When a man does his work to the best of his ability . . ."

He did. Absolutely. Down to the tiniest detail. At this moment he was even walking at the same pace as his father used to walk, with Blanche on his right, his son on his left, a little way behind, with that Sunday afternoon gait, with that rapt, dedicated look characteristic of devout churchgoers walking behind the Holy Sacrament.

At thirty-five, Blanche was no longer attractive, if she ever had been. Did she still have any sex appeal? At fifty she would be an old woman, and at sixty her figure would have gone to pieces and she would have fat, shapeless legs like most of those women he used to see, in slippers now that they could no longer get into their shoes, doing their shopping in Rue des Francs-Bourgeois.

He was happy. . . . They were all happy. . . . They had to be, otherwise there was no longer such a thing as justice. . . .

They were walking across the site of the development, past the concrete units, full of eyes looking down at them, following their progress as one follows an insect threading its way among the grass.

They were out for a breath of air. They were inspecting

82

the new setting of their life. Was it so wretched or so discouraging?

What did they use to do, those other Sundays? Every other one, they went to Kremlin, taking a tart for tea, because his father liked tarts, especially bilberry tarts.

They didn't talk much, and what they did say was not always answered. His father had become hard of hearing. You almost had to shout. You didn't dare look at the clock with the brass pendulum. As for the garden, it had shrunk with time and the leaves were covered with dust.

They were happy.

On other Sundays, the car took them thirty or sixty miles out of Paris, wedging itself into a line of cars full of bad-tempered or impatient children.

"When do we get there?"

"Will we be able to fish?"

Alain had got past the stage of questions like that and merely drew back in a corner, with a sullen look on his face. They found a patch of grass to picnic on, or they went to a small restaurant off a side road.

"How many people do you think there are living here by now?"

He gave a start, and repeated to himself the question which Blanche had just asked.

"I don't know. Fifteen hundred? Two thousand?"

"Are they going on building?"

"They have plans for ten new houses. Look! Here's where the swimming pool's going to be."

Blanche couldn't swim. He himself was a bad swimmer. In his day, a good student didn't have much time to devote to sports. And he was forced to be a good student.

Then a good employee, a good husband, a good father, a good manager. There had never been any transgression!

What for?

Did his neighbor have any sense of responsibility or didn't he care? Perhaps he had no conscience at all.

Blanche was full of admiration, because she was supposed to admire it all. And also to give him pleasure, because it was he who was to a certain extent responsible for their exodus.

"I had no idea that we were so near real country."

They had reached the wheatfield.

"Did you see the poppies and the cornflowers? Don't they remind you of something?"

But of course! Their first Sunday walk. He had picked her a few cornflowers, which she had stuck in the buttonhole of her blouse. After fifteen years, she was still grateful and let him know this by a long, tender glance.

"Isn't that enough of a walk?" Alain said impatiently.

At his age, Emile hadn't liked Sunday walks either, but he didn't dare show it. Curiously, when he looked back on them now, it was with nostalgia, as if he were thinking of a paradise lost.

Was it because of this that he imposed them on his son? Or simply because it was family tradition?

"We could have gone to the movies."

"On a lovely day like this?"

It was essential to make the most of the fine weather, to breathe in the clean air.

They discovered, to the left, a road which was new to them. Fields and pastureland stretched away on both sides and, on a hillock, they saw a real farm, with cows grazing all around, and a hayrick. Blanche was in ecstasies:

"It's real countryside!"

They walked on and very soon caught sight of a slender steeple which seemed to rise out of the ground, then the square tower of a tiny church, and its gray slate roof.

Soon low-built houses appeared in the landscape, most

of them painted white, a solitary one in a vivid red, not laid out in streets but set down at random. Each had its little garden, a few flowers, rows of leeks, young peas, and green beans climbing up their poles.

An old man in shirt-sleeves stopped digging and mopped his brow on his sleeve as he watched them go by.

"Do you know the village?"

"It's more like a hamlet. We must look at the map. No one's ever told me about it."

"Look."

A real country grocer's, a dark, narrow, deep shop which sold everything, starch and sweets, candles and canned goods, knitting wool and overalls.

"When I can't find what I want at Fairview, I'll know where to go."

A little beyond the church, the word "Café" stood out on the wall of a house slightly different from the rest.

"Are you thirsty?"

Jovis was getting excited. By accident they had discovered a finishing point to their stroll, a touch of the picturesque.

"Sure I'm thirsty," answered Alain.

The door was open and a reddish-brown dog took its time before getting up from the entrance to let them pass. In the semidarkness four men were playing cards. There were only three tables in all, and an odd kind of counter with an enormous green plant in a pink china cachepot.

One of the card players got up almost as laboriously as the reddish-brown dog.

"What would you like to drink?"

"A lemonade," answered Alain.

"What about you, Blanche?"

"Anything you say. You know, I . . ."

She was never thirsty. She was never hungry. She was always given too much, and she never failed to say thank you. . . .

"How's your white wine?"

"It's what we drink."

There was a bottle on the card table where the players were waiting, their cards in their hands, as in a picture, just beneath a copy of the law governing drunk and disorderly behavior.

"A pint?"

"Yes, that'll be enough for us both."

They might have been hundreds of miles from Paris, or even fifty years back in the past.

They sat down at one of the tables and the men returned to their game, which Emile wasn't familiar with. A woman half opened the glass kitchen door to look at them; she was a real countrywoman, again straight out of a picture, her breasts sagging over an enormous stomach, dressed in black with white trimmings. On one cheek she even had a wart with some hairs sticking out of it.

"I'm happy. . . . I'm . . ."

He was poking fun at himself, irritated with his state of mind. Had he acquired so little maturity, in the space of thirty-five years, that he was thrown off balance by a slight change in his environment?

After all, they hadn't gone off to the Congo or to China. They had merely made the small jump from Rue des Francs-Bourgeois to these new buildings which had gone up on the outskirts of Paris.

True, he had been nervous about Blanche at the beginning. He thought then that Blanche might get bored, left alone at home, against a less lively and more stand-offish background than that of old Paris.

But it was she who had shrugged that aside first. She had

hardly arrived before she had found something to occupy her, and very soon she would be showing them proudly, a little as if it was all her own work, the outside of the day nursery, closed on Sundays, and especially the lawn surrounded by the white railings where one could watch the children playing.

Hadn't Alain himself, this very morning, made a new friend?

"I'm happy, for God's . . ."

No! He never swore, not even in his thoughts. It was stronger than he. It was part of his education and he endeavored to instill it into his son in his turn.

Had she succeeded so well with him?

Only a few foul words had been needed, a few noises and groans, some all too evocative cries the other side of the wall, to trouble him as much as if he had discovered something really terrifying.

And indeed he had. He knew that such words existed; he had heard them spoken by boys at school, he had read them in public lavatories. He had a theoretical knowledge of such ways of making love, gathered from books he had read on the sly and from newspaper stories. All that frenzy, madness, bestiality . . . They even talked about it in the Bible! . . .

But to know that in the same building, separated from him, from his wife, from his son, from their life, from their beliefs, from their taboos, by a mere partition, there were human beings who indulged in . . .

Why, suddenly, this craving to learn more about it, to listen, to get closer to these people?

Because he had watched out for them three nights running, forcing himself to stay awake even though ordinarily he set so much store by his sleep, and had been disappointed when nothing happened, or only fairly ordinary things.

He had seen the man, taller than he, stronger than he, more handsome than he. He did not impress one as being unhappy, undermined by vice and by remorse. He exuded health and a relaxed, free life through every pore.

The woman, although he had seen only her back and her hair, was probably just as good-looking.

If he had met them somewhere else, he wouldn't have had any doubts about them. Behind his counter, he would have greeted them enthusiastically and tried to sell them the most expensive holidays possible.

Though their son was on the fat side and much like a dummy, Alain, so choosy about his friends, had already adopted him.

Who was right, then?

The man didn't get up at half-past six to go off to the office. He slept late every morning, with an enticing woman beside him, in a bed which Emile imagined covered in frills and furbelows like a courtesan's couch.

Did their son go to school, to the lycée? Probably. He had obviously had a motor scooter for a long time. He hadn't been made to wait for years, not only for reasons of expense but for fear of an accident.

He had all the records he wanted. In a few days' time, he would be a sort of hero in Alain's eyes, an ideal which he would try hard to emulate.

Would Jovis ever have thought of wearing nothing but shorts on a Sunday morning, parading his bare torso on the terrace like that?

Admittedly it was nothing, just a commonplace detail, but he knew the importance of such details.

He knew himself as well. If he was so disturbed, so annoyed with himself, it was because it was not the first time that he had gone through a crisis and because, each time, it had ended in a welter of bitterness and shame.

He was happy. . . .

Was he happy, for example, when he was eighteen, supposedly the best year of one's life, when he was working at Maître Depoux's and was treated by him as if he were a servant in spite of having just passed his examination so brilliantly?

He thought he had a future, an immediate future, guaranteed by his diploma, and he was spending his days in an office looking out on an evil-smelling courtyard.

He had run away. Just as he was to run away later, because each time it was real flight, from the import business on Rue du Caire.

Even when he was with the Barillon Travel Agency, when he was first taken on in the Boulevard Poissonnière office, he had been disappointed and used to read the help wanted column in the paper every evening.

He learned English, German, Spanish. He learned bookkeeping. He wanted to know everything, to help him climb more quickly. . . .

To run further away, to climb higher?

At last they recognized his abilities. Monsieur Armand appointed him to the Bastille office and, two years later, it was he who replaced the manager when he died from a stroke in his office.

The offices were redecorated. It was as if he were master of it all. He moved, choosing a light apartment, without flowered wallpaper, without dusty recesses, without the sweat of many generations of tenants.

The wine was too sweet, but Blanche drank it with pleasure.

"Don't you like it?"

"Yes, I do."

A canary was hopping about in a cage.

"Check, please."

They were annoying the players, who must have imagined that they had come in only out of curiosity.

Monsieur Armand, for instance . . . He was an important person. . . . He was married and had two sons. . . . He owned a large house in the woods of Saint-Germain, a few miles from Versailles, to which he drove out every evening. . . . He traveled a lot, to establish contacts. . . .

However, when he went off on his business trips, it was with his secretary, who was under twenty-five. He was more or less sure that he had bought her an apartment in the six-teenth *arrondissement,* though he had another affair of long standing.

The employees knew about it. His friends must know about it too. In the Champs-Elysées offices, where there was a large staff, most of the women employees had slept with him. They didn't mind. On the contrary, it was they who made the advances.

No one criticized him. He remained a respectable, prosperous man. Perhaps, in some bedroom, in some bed, he carried on like the neighbor with the red car?

"Shall we go back?"

"As you like."

"I think there might be a storm."

Because the sky seemed overcast to the west and the south.

"Shall we ask the name of the village?"

He questioned the old man who was digging and who raised his straw hat.

"The name? Good God, you're in it and you don't know its name? It's Rancourt, of course. But it's not a village. There isn't a town hall or a school. The township is down there, near the Boisrond farm."

"Are you two walking so slowly on purpose, Daddy?"

No. It was a Sunday speed. They were out for a walk. There wasn't anything waiting for them.

"Are you in a hurry?"

"It makes me tired."

"We'll walk faster. You're not tired, are you, Blanche?"

"Of course not."

They met only one other couple. The woman was pushing a baby carriage. They looked at one another, hesitating whether to make some sign of greeting. In the country, people do greet one another. But what about housing developments?

He kept on ending up with that word, and couldn't think of another however much he tried. Even so, it is disturbing not to be able to define the place one lives in.

"Where do you live?"

"Fairview."

"Where's that? What is it?"

"It's . . ."

What was it? A group of buildings. Some blocks of concrete with bedrooms, living rooms, bathrooms, and kitchens.

He had not admitted to himself what he was searching for from the moment they had started this walk; he was trying to deceive himself, to put himself off the scent.

What he had really wanted was to go and see the Carillon Doré, to come to terms with himself, to give shape and substance to the names he had heard pronounced: Alexa, Irène, Yolande . . .

Because there was a Yolande as well; his neighbor had talked about her the third night and clearly treated her as he treated the others. Yolande was the youngest and the least professional. Irène was a nice girl, standing up in the telephone booth. Alexa, on the other hand, was sufficiently complex for Farran's wife to be interested in her movements and gestures and to copy them.

91

He needed a complete picture. Those words which he had overheard created images that had no connection with everyday life. When he could see, when he knew, he would undoubtedly say to himself:

"That's all there is to it!"

He couldn't suggest to Blanche that he should take her to a night club.

"Can you see me in a place like that, Emile? With my figure and dowdy clothes?"

She wouldn't understand him going there alone. He must find an excuse. In the old days, when he was taking his evening courses, it was easy, but he hadn't profited by it, except once, and then he hadn't gone all the way.

It did happen that he had to stay in the office, at the height of the season, until eight o'clock, occasionally until nine, with the shutters closed, straightening out files, but he had never got home later than nine-thirty.

"Why didn't we go and see Grandfather?"

"Because I wanted to show your mother around here, I told you."

"There's not very much to see, is there?"

Was he like that when he had been the same age as his son? He sincerely wondered. Deep down, he finally admitted it to himself, he used to think in much the same way, but he didn't dare say it. Not only because of the way he had been brought up, or the respect children were made to feel then. He had been frightened of distressing people. He still was. He often caught himself watching his wife and his son.

"Is he happy? . . . Is she happy? . . ."

The slightest clouding on a face worried him. If they weren't happy, it could only be his fault, since he was responsible for them.

And what about him? What about his happiness? Who was responsible for that? Who attended to that?

Not Alain, of course. He was too young and thought only of himself.

Blanche, yes. She did what she could. She did it so obviously that it became oppressive and boring.

She was not only his wife. One could say that she was his wife only in addition to everything else. She was his mother, his sister, and his servant all at once. She was on the go from morning till night and ended up by falling asleep immediately, her mouth half open, like someone who has done her duty and can't do another thing.

It was not especially for him. She would no doubt have done the same with another man, because it was in her, a need to devote herself, to sacrifice herself.

She was about to devote herself to children she didn't know, because her two men, Emile and Alain, didn't need her enough any more. If she had had an ill or disabled person to look after, she would have done it with the same zest.

He had chosen her. Would he, in full awareness of what it meant, have chosen a woman like the one in the next-door apartment? Could he have put himself on the same wavelength and have given a supreme importance to his sexual life?

Farran did it and was in better shape than he!

A tourist plane passed a bare two hundred yards above their heads, and the pilot watched them walking along the red ribbon of the road.

An airplane . . . A customer who . . . An important customer . . .

He set himself to inventing the story. An important customer had booked his seat on a flight for the United States, or for Japan, Japan would be better, he must consult the timetables.

He had forgotten his passport . . . No, not his passport . . . His briefcase . . . He had left his briefcase at the

93

office and they didn't know which hotel he was staying at
. . . An American . . . Jovis had to meet him at the airport to return his briefcase, which contained important
documents, perhaps traveler's checks . . .

He smiled faintly with satisfaction. It was not so difficult, after all. He had just solved the problem.

He went over to break off an ear of wheat.

"Would you like it?" he asked Blanche, holding it out
to her. "Did you also nibble the seeds when you were young?
They're still quite warm from the sun. It smells of rising
dough. . . ."

Alain, saying nothing and walking along with his eyes on
the ground, probably thought they were ridiculous.

Chapter Five

THAT day was at the same time one of the longest and one of the shortest of his whole life. Since the day before, when he had made the decision, he had been in a hurry to put it into execution and, as the time passed, he was seized with a kind of dizziness.

He would have liked it to happen immediately, and at the same time he was afraid. From early morning, on the terrace of the bar on Place des Vosges, after he had driven Alain to the Lycée Charlemagne, he had been overcome with sudden pangs, his forehead broke out in sweat, his hands began to tremble faintly.

Why did he need to go to the Carillon Doré, to penetrate, almost as if he were a housebreaker, an unknown world with which he had no connection?

For he realized that there was something aggressive and underhanded about the projected visit to the night club on Rue Ponthieu. He was not going as an ordinary customer. His intention was to spy.

To spy out what? The girls, whom he knew only by their

Christian names and, because of his neighbor's words, by their ways of making love?

Farran, sitting on a stool at the bar opposite the man called Léon?

There was the story about the cars, cars which were probably stolen, "lifted" by Little Louis.

Like everybody else, he had read stories about criminals, girls, drugs, repainted cars, trafficking of all kinds which took place in certain bars that were open at night.

From time to time one learned that there had been a settling of accounts, that someone had been killed entering or leaving one of those places.

He was an honest man. He had never crossed the dividing line between good and evil.

That didn't stack up. It wasn't the visit to the Carillon which didn't stack up, it was the excuse which he had hit on the previous day for not returning home.

It barely took ten minutes by car between his apartment and Orly Airport. If he had had a briefcase to return to some American, nothing would have prevented him from having dinner with his wife and son, from spending the evening watching television, from making the short trip to Orly, where he would have needed only an hour to find his customer.

"Waiter, another one."

That was becoming a habit, almost a vice, and this morning he ordered, at the last minute, a third glass of Pouilly which gave him a certain sense of well-being but increased his agitation.

Raising the iron shutters at the agency, he felt guilty. He hadn't done anything yet. He would certainly do nothing wrong. He had no intention of doing so. It would still be the first time he had lied to Blanche.

Monday morning was always very busy, because most

tradesmen kept their shops closed and made the most of it by coming to discuss their travel arrangements or their next vacations.

Joseph Remacle asked him:

"Do I go to Orly, Monsieur Jovis?"

He had forgotten the special flight. Societies, sports clubs, sometimes chartered an entire plane for a journey. This was the case today. Rather a curious case, really, as it concerned a group of former shopkeepers in Boulevard Beaumarchais.

They numbered about forty old men and women who had spent their whole lives next door to one another and who, now that they were no longer young and had sold their businesses, had decided not to lose contact. Some of them still lived in the district. Others were scattered about Paris, in the suburbs, and even in the country.

As a rule they met once a month for a reunion dinner in a brasserie on Place de la Republique, and once a year they took a trip together.

This time they had chartered a plane to take them on a tour of the Mediterranean, and the flight was due to leave at eleven o'clock. The agency, in cases like that, felt itself responsible and an employee always went to Orly to make sure that all was well.

"Yes, you do, Remacle. Be at the airport a good hour before the plane leaves. There are bound to be some in the group who've never flown before."

He had just hit upon the solution. A chartered plane, that was it.

He would invent one which would ostensibly leave toward midnight, for example, or about one in the morning. All he would need to do would be to telephone his wife toward the end of the afternoon. No! He was forgetting poor Alain, whom he must drive back to Fairview.

He would see. He had enough time to think about it,

between customers, to get his story worked out. Alain bothered him the most. He didn't want to go to Fairview before his visit to Rue de Ponthieu; he was afraid that, once he was home, he wouldn't have the courage.

Still, it was necessary. He didn't know why it was necessary, but he felt it was.

Like a need to see, to touch.

He didn't like big words, but one has to admit that good and evil do exist. Up to the first night at Fairview, his idea of evil had hardly been a very attractive one, almost hideous, a little like paintings of Hell.

But the devil he had just encountered did not have that kind of face. After the turbulent nights, the indecent words, the frolics which he knew about down to the least detail but which he refused to conjure up, he saw again Farran on the balcony, fair-haired, smiling, in shorts, lighting his cigarette with a lighter which was probably gold.

Was that the image of one of the damned as it is pictured by someone who has been brought up in Kremlin-Bicêtre by a schoolmaster-father, who has married Blanche and who has always been a model employee, taking evening courses?

Nor did the woman, in her silk dressing gown with its tiny flowers, with her supple brown hair falling over her shoulders, look the least like one of the damned.

He hadn't made out what they were saying on Sunday morning, but their voices were untroubled, gay, and it was also an untroubled Walter who had gone down for a walk.

He absolutely had to . . .

He would have preferred to do it at once. He was afraid that, as the day slipped by, his courage would abandon him. Soon, perhaps, he would consider the project ridiculous and give it up?

"Hello! . . . Yes, I can hear you . . . No . . .

There's no direct line . . . The plane stops over at Rome, but there's only an hour's waiting time . . . Not at all . . . I'll give you further details when you come and pick up your ticket . . . Yes, it's ready . . . First class . . ."

He lunched alone in his bistro on Rue Jacques-Coeur. He did not realize what he was eating. Luckily, Monsieur Armand would be coming to the agency at about three to talk over certain projects with him, and that would keep him busy for most of two hours.

Too bad! He would have to fit Alain in, as he wouldn't have the nerve to put him on a bus.

He came to the office, as on the other days, looked at the posters while he was waiting for his father, then the two of them went to find the car parked on the other side of the square.

"Eight more days . . ."

There were only eight more days before the school holidays. Then he would have to take Blanche and his son to Dieppe, where he would spend the weekends with them. Usually, it wasn't too unpleasant for him to be alone. He organized for himself the restricted existence of a bachelor or of a widower, and it did not lack charm.

This time, he was at a loss. On Rue des Francs-Bourgeois things were easy. But how would it go in the new apartment, which he hadn't got used to yet? He had tried out his armchair in three different corners of the living room, and the most recent arrangement of the furniture was by no means final.

"Did the work go well?"

"We're doing very little right now."

"What did he talk to you about yesterday, your new friend?"

"He's not a friend."

"Is he nice?"

"I don't know yet."

"Does he go to the Villejuif lycée?"

"I didn't ask him. I told you yesterday: we talked mainly about jazz."

His insistence irritated the boy, who didn't like being interrogated about what he considered to be his own sphere. Did he question his father about what he did at the office, or his mother about the dolls at the day nursery?

The red car was not outside the apartment house. They did not see Walter at the window.

Dinner was ready, and he didn't dare refuse to eat with his wife and son. He regretted it. He had hoped that he might dine in town, by himself in a corner of the restaurant, so as to prepare himself gradually.

"I've got to go out, my dears."

It was so unexpected that they both looked at him, their forks suspended in mid-air.

"A group of important people, financial experts, have to go off to Japan on urgent business. I haven't got a crystal ball, but I suspect that a big Japanese bank with French interests tied up in it is about to fail. . . ."

He was finicking. He was being too elaborate.

"I couldn't get them on one of the regular flights. I've organized a special flight for them, which wasn't easy with such little warning, especially in the vacation season."

"Are you going to Orly? Can I come with you?"

Alain was excited already.

"No, I'm not going to Orly right away. First I must go to the office and wait for full particulars, then on to the head office. Also I must inform all the people concerned that I shall be at the airport an hour before take-off."

"When do you think you'll get back?"

"Probably not before two in the morning."

100

He hadn't blushed. He was surprised to feel so much at his ease in the midst of lying to his wife and son in this way.

"It's a big thing for the agency."

He wiped his lips and got up.

"Sleep well, my dears. I'll try not to make a noise when I come in."

Just as he was getting into the car, while Blanche was leaning on the balustrade, he saw the red convertible drive up, and this annoyed him. The man got out and walked toward the entrance of the building without appearing to notice his presence.

Why shouldn't Farran have dinner at home before going off to the night club? Unless it was closed one day a week, like many restaurants, and that day was precisely Monday?

Once he was on the throughway, he drove faster than usual, as if it were in his power to speed up the passing of time. He was in a hurry to know.

To know what?

It was no longer important. He didn't ask himself questions. What mattered was reaching the Carillon Doré, going in, seeing.

He drove around the vicinity of the Champs-Elysées for a long time looking for a place to park before he remembered that there was a garage under Avenue George V.

He began to walk, looking at his watch. It wasn't nine o'clock in the evening yet, and surely the night club wouldn't open before eleven or midnight.

At the corner of Rue Washington, a young girl glanced at him questioningly, as if she were waiting for a sign from him. Did he look like a man who goes up to women like that? When he walked past her, she shrugged her shoulders and took up her post again.

He walked around for twenty minutes, and finally went into

a movie house. The usherette, it seemed to him, also looked at him closely, as if she expected him to ask her something. To put him next to a pretty girl, perhaps?

It was a war movie; there were some deafening passages, because of the guns, the planes, the machine guns which were firing full blast. Men covered in mud, their rifles aimed toward the front, followed one another in Indian file into a swamp.

He had made a mistake in saying that he would go to the office. Supposing his wife wanted to speak to him, she would telephone there and no one would answer.

It was ridiculous. She had never had anything urgent to let him know. There was no reason why Alain should get hurt or Blanche should suddenly become ill.

Except for the troublesome period after her confinement, she had never been ill and he couldn't remember seeing her spend a single day in bed. Even when she had flu, she refused to take her temperature and went on with the household chores.

She was happy, wasn't she? They were all happy!

What difference would it make if he yielded to a spurt of curiosity and pushed open the door of a night club?

He found himself in the streets at the time when all the movie houses were disgorging their audiences onto the sidewalks, and it took him a moment to get his bearings. Now there were three women on the corner of Rue Washington, and they seemed to understand one another perfectly.

It didn't worry them, plying their trade one in front of the other. One of them was young, still fresh-looking. She smiled at him and he almost smiled back, out of politeness, so as not to upset her.

Rue de Ponthieu was more lively than during the day. Neon signs, red, blue, yellow, or green, indicated night clubs, bars, and restaurants.

As he approached the Carillon Doré he almost stopped breathing, and he had to make an effort to put out his arm toward the doorknob and to push it.

"Your hat, monsieur . . ."

A girl in a very short skirt was in charge of the cloakroom in a corner set off by a railing. To the left he saw a mahogany bar and some stools, nearly all of which were occupied.

The lights, tangerine-colored as people used to say, were so subdued that he had to get used to the semidarkness.

"A good table, monsieur?"

The headwaiter was trying to draw him toward the center of the room where some tables, each one with a champagne bucket and a bottle with a big gold cork, were placed around a tiny floor.

He nearly let himself be drawn along, but turned toward the bar, and saw a free stool next to one occupied by a woman in a yellow dress.

"I prefer to stay here."

"As you like."

"Missed!" the headwaiter seemed to say to himself, like the girl on the corner of Rue Washington just before.

He climbed onto the stool. The barman wiped the bar in front of him with a napkin, and looked at him questioningly.

"What would you like?"

"Can I have half a pint of beer?"

"I'm sorry, we haven't got any beer. Only champagne, whisky, gin, and vodka."

Everyone must realize that this was the first time he had set foot in a place of this sort, and his neighbor turned her head to hide a smile, perhaps to wink at Léon.

A Léon who was rather small, chubby, and pink, whom one might have met anywhere. Jovis thought he looked like a hairdresser.

"Whisky," he murmured.

He had only drunk it two or three times, for instance on Remacle's birthday, when Remacle had offered everyone in the office whisky in a bar near the Bastille. He didn't like the taste, but it wasn't as strong as he had anticipated.

He watched the yellowish liquid being poured into his glass.

"Soda water?"

"Yes, please."

"Let me have another, Léon."

His neighbor had turned in his direction and kept on glancing at him with curiosity.

As for him, he was looking out for Farran, astonished at not seeing him. There were mainly men at the bar, except for his neighbor and a brunette, in a gold dress, leaning on the other end. Why did he decide that that one was Alexa? She had a skin-tight dress and she could not possibly be wearing anything under it. He wondered how she managed to get it on and take it off.

Her body was strong and supple, soft, no doubt, but firm beneath the touch. Their eyes met. She didn't smile at him, but he read curiosity in her look.

Had they never before seen a man like him at the Carillon? Three of the customers, at the bar, were younger and were discussing something that had to do with the movies. Jovis didn't catch every word, merely gathered that it was a question of estimates, of guaranteed distribution, of a co-production with the Germans.

When he took a cigarette from his pocket, Léon held the flame of a match out to him at the same time as his neighbor lit a lighter.

He hesitated between the two flames and, as the barman seemed the more important person, it was the match he chose.

The woman laughed.

"That's not being very nice to me."

"I beg your pardon. I didn't realize at once that . . ."

"It doesn't matter. Do you come here often?"

She knew he didn't, since they didn't know each other and she had undoubtedly been working at the establishment for some time.

"It's the first time."

He mustn't cheat. They would realize at once and would distrust him. His conscience wasn't clear, and he thought of himself rather as some kind of spy.

"Do you come from Paris?"

"Yes. More or less. I moved outside Paris a few days ago."

"You're lucky."

She wasn't being provocative. She was talking gently to him, without putting herself out. There was nothing exceptional about her face. She was neither beautiful nor ugly, just natural and pleasant, without any complications.

Why was it the other girl, the one he supposed to be Alexa, whom he was watching over his shoulder?

"Chin-chin!"

He repeated, ashamed of pronouncing such ridiculous words:

"Chin-chin!"

If his father . . . If his wife . . .

She emptied her glass in one draught.

"Do you like Scotch?"

"Not much. I prefer beer."

"So do I. Besides, I come from Alsace. From Strasbourg. Do you know Strasbourg?"

"I've been there twice."

"Did you eat at L'Aubette?"

He was going to answer in the negative when, in the mirror

which hung behind the rows of bottles, he recognized the face and broad shoulders of his neighbor at Fairview. Farran was standing motionless, talking in an undertone to the head-waiter, looking all around the room and the bar, observing each customer, acting the role of the proprietor.

As he threaded his way to rejoin the woman in the gold dress, he rapped out:

"Hello, Irène."

"Hello, Jean."

As he passed he cast an indifferent glance at Jovis, and the very next moment he planted a brief kiss on the neck of the girl who was surely Alexa.

There were still a few couples dancing on the floor when the band suddenly stopped playing. There was a roll of drums, the lights went out, and some bluish spotlights picked out as if from nowhere a red-haired woman in a turn-of-the-century costume.

The band was now playing "Viens Poupoule" and the woman was circling the floor in a series of little dance steps, patting a bald-headed man sitting within arm's reach as she passed him, with the tip of her fan.

The customers at the tables watched her with their eyes popping; the men and women at the bar, more indifferent, accorded the turn only vague attention and carried on their conversations in an undertone.

"That's Mabel," whispered Irène. "She used to dance the can-can at the Tabarin before they pulled it down to build a garage."

She was wearing an extravagantly flowered hat, a period dress with a false hoop or pannier in iridescent silk, and a feather boa around her neck. When she hitched up her skirts at each entrechat, she revealed high black leather boots.

"She's the only real dancer here, but her breasts aren't good enough and they make her go on first."

She talked in a flat voice, dispassionately, without envy.

"I'm going to get ready, as I'm on after her. See you soon."

This was her way of arranging some sort of rendezvous with him, and it embarrassed him because he had made no move in that direction. All he had done was to answer her questions. Their content had been perfectly simple, and not in the least equivocal.

"Have a good time, dear."

He searched for Farran, and met his eyes staring at him. Perhaps it was only a fluke. Jovis turned away, and a little later it was Alexa who seemed to be watching him.

On the floor, Mabel had thrown her feather boa toward the audience and was unbuttoning her dress; a few moments later it fell at her feet. She was wearing voluminous under-clothes, very full and old-fashioned, and now it was the turn of her petticoats, then her camisole.

The music played. More little steps as she danced around, silent jokes with the spectators in the first row.

Thinking of the scene between Irène and Farran, he looked for the telephone booth. Public telephone booths usually have a glass door, so that anyone passing . . .

He was astonished that the girl who had been sitting beside him a moment ago could have done such a thing. She was completely straightforward, talking to him as if he were a friend. It was true that, for the people here, making love must be commonplace.

The four musicians wore striped waistcoats. Because of the spotlights one could hardly distinguish their faces. The dancer moved toward the bald-headed customer whose head she had tapped with her fan and invited him to unlace her corset.

He got up, with a foolish smile on his face. She rubbed up

107

against him. He was a man of sixty, spruce, elegantly dressed, who must be someone important in public life, a director or associate director. Tomorrow he would reprimand an employee who had come in late, or a tired typist.

While she took off her scalloped panties, the woman accompanied the movement with a show of shocked modesty, but she still had on a transparent lawn chemise.

One more round. She faced them, halted, turned her back. The chemise flew over her head at the same moment as the music stopped.

Jovis felt a tightening of the throat at the sight of the naked body, of the back, of the buttocks. He wondered whether the woman was going to turn around. No, of course not! The spotlights went out, the lights were turned on. She had disappeared.

He was not sexually excited. He would have been hard put to it to say what was going on inside him. He was embarrassed at being here, for a start, like the bald-headed man, like the others who had followed the headwaiter toward the first row.

"Another?"

He turned around. The barman was holding the bottle over his glass and he didn't dare say no.

"How about Mademoiselle Irène?"

This detail shocked him. The whole thing was organized. Some of them were in a conspiracy to squeeze as much money as possible out of the customers, and he, Jovis, was one of these customers.

This did not keep him from being prey to a special excitement, caused by the music, the lighting, the presence beside him, just now, of a girl he hadn't known the day before and also, in spite of everything, of this nude woman who had become, under the glare of the spotlights, a kind of symbol.

The groans, the words wrenched from the woman behind

the wall, came back into his mind, her harsh voice, the occasional sound like a death-rattle.

One would have said that, for her, love was a shaking, dramatic experience, a cult with rites which had to be followed to the ultimate end.

Only Farran preserved his calmness and his irony. Where was he off to now? He passed near Jovis, threading his way, and reached a small door near the cloakroom. The next moment a fresh roll of drums was the signal for a new act, and it was Irène who was revealed after the few seconds of traditional darkness.

She looked like a sweet young girl, and this disturbed Jovis further. He might have had a daughter instead of a son. As far as he could make out, at that distance and in that lighting, she looked barely fourteen, about the same age as Alain.

He was tempted to leave. He had seen. Did he need to learn anything more? He turned toward the bar and met the eyes of Léon, who seemed to be ordering him to stay.

It was absurd! The plump little man wasn't saying a word and his blue eyes were devoid of any particular expression. Even so, Jovis would not have dared to say:

"Check, please."

Besides, he felt obliged to watch Irène after she had spoken so nicely to him. By now her breasts were bare, the small round breasts of a young girl. He had the impression that she was searching for him with her eyes and that she was making some kind of sign to him.

She did not turn around, like the first dancer. When she let drop her last piece of clothing, she boldly faced the audience, but her pubis, which ought to have been blonde like her hair, was veiled by a triangle of black silk.

The barman applauded. Emile felt himself obliged to applaud as well while Irène was threading her way toward a door at the back. Alexa was no longer in her place at the end of the bar. He was astonished to see her again, a few moments later, sheathed in black, in the middle of the floor, welcomed by applause.

There was a voice in his ear:

"She's the star show."

Irène was back, and she seized her glass as she murmured:

"It's nice of you to have got me a drink."

"Don't mention it!"

Alexa, stretched out on a Madame Récamier-style chaise longue, seemed to be in a daydream. Before an imaginary mirror she was admiring the line of her body, emphasizing it with her hand, caressing her breasts, her stomach, her thighs, in a show of ecstasy.

"She's quite something, don't you think?"

"I'm not a good judge."

He was submitting, without being really in it. Everything was unfolding outside him and he did not have the feeling of really being at the bar with a woman whom he did not know and who treated him like an old friend.

She dropped her shoe and he hesitated to pick it up, then he did and put it back on her foot, which forced him to touch her ankle.

He did not feel any sexual excitement, perhaps because this was the very reaction she wanted to arouse in him, in everyone who was there as a customer.

His particular excitement was different. He watched the barman as he watched Farran, who had just reappeared and was standing with his back to the door. The cloakroom girl was motionless at her post, as were the headwaiter, the waiters.

He felt he was at the hub of an organization which fascinated him and frightened him somewhat. Everything was going like well-oiled clockwork. They hardly needed to whisper a word in one another's ear. Imperceptible signs were enough. Each one, in his place, played his own role automatically.

He was only an intruder . . . Not even a customer . . . Because he wasn't a real customer, which must be obvious from his attitude and behavior . . .

"You'll soon see when she goes into her orgasm . . ."

He gave a start, and looked sharply at Irène, who had said this as if it were the most natural thing in the world.

"I don't mean that she really goes into an orgasm . . . But, that's what the show is . . ."

It was true. The atmosphere was becoming denser, the silence deeper, anguished, punctuated by occasional runs on the bass.

It was part of the rite. Alexa's face, drained of blood, was thrown back, her purple lips opened in a grin, and her body was twisting in the grip of pain and pleasure.

He was about to speak. His companion motioned to him to remain silent. Even the bar regulars had stopped their low-pitched conversations. Everyone was watching anxiously, waiting for the release.

It was sham, it was cheap, granted, but that didn't stop it from being light-years away from his hardworking, decent life. If he had suddenly seen Blanche standing in front of him, even his son Alain, he would probably not have given them a single glance.

Irène's hand clenched his shoulder and he did not find the gesture embarrassing. Was it her state of nerves which made her dig her nails right into his skin? He hardly felt it.

A final spasm and Alexa leaped onto the floor. Then, in the midst of the applause and the relieved cheering, she took off, as a kind of acknowledgment, her black sheath and waved it above her head like a flag.

Lights came on, this time as golden as her skin.

"She's beautiful, don't you think?"

She had just called him *"tu."* She slipped from her stool and murmured:

"Come on . . ."

He had no time to hesitate, to reflect. Even so, he knew. They were playing with him as if he were a puppet. It was all phony.

No. It was not all so false since, when he got home, Farran and his wife . . .

"What did she do to you?"

He followed Irène toward the cloakroom, without really knowing where she was leading him. She didn't make for the door against which Farran was still leaning, but for the exit.

"We'll be back very soon," she said to the girl who was looking for Jovis's hat or pretending to look for it.

They were out on the sidewalk. It was strange to see the passers-by, the shopwindows, the street, the houses, but Irène was already going through the adjacent door with the word "Studios" above it.

"It's very nice here, you'll see."

They went up in the elevator, crossed a hallway, and the young woman called out to some invisible person:

"I'm going to number four."

He did not expect to find himself in a modern drawing room, decorated in good taste, with a bottle of champagne waiting for them in a bucket.

"Open it, will you? I'm dying of thirst! Really, I've never liked whisky, it always leaves a nasty taste in my mouth."

She looked at herself in a mirror, and touched up her eyes with a little blue eye-shadow.

"Have you never been here? Wait. I'll come and help you."

It was she who opened the bottle.

"You're married, aren't you? I'm sure your wife is pretty.

Perhaps prettier than me. Admit that you'd rather have gone with Alexa!"

He tried to protest.

"Ssh! I saw how you were looking at her. It's the same with all the men. I'm only the appetizer. Next time, you'll have Alexa. I'll try not to disappoint you too much. Aren't you drinking?"

"Yes, thank you."

It was too late to back out without hurting her, without perhaps creating an incident with the lessees of the apartment, or with Farran whom he suspected of being the owner of the Carillon.

"Don't you like me?"

"I do."

"My number isn't perfect yet. I'll have to work some more at it, but we have to change it every now and then. There are regulars, some who come two or three times a week, invariably for Alexa."

"Who was that, the tall fair man who was with her at the bar just now?"

"I don't know. One of her friends, I suppose."

"Does he too come here often?"

"Now and then."

She was lying. That annoyed him. She refilled the glasses and invited him to drink once more.

"Don't you find it hot in here? Do you mind?"

She took off her dress, under which she was only wearing briefs and a bra.

"Aren't you going to undress?"

Turning her back on him, she leaned over a sofa which with a few practiced movements she transformed into a bed.

"Wait, I'll help you."

She undid his tie and unbuttoned his shirt.

"Where did you say you lived?"

"Just outside Paris."

"In the suburbs?"

"Not exactly. A little farther out."

With the tips of her nails, she was tracing arabesques on his naked skin, and he shivered.

"Don't you want me?"

He answered clumsily:

"I don't know."

He was annoyed with this phrase, with this acceptance.

"Really, you're a wonderful man."

"Why?"

"Because one can read in your face everything you're thinking."

"What am I thinking?"

"You're frightened of me. Come on! Have another glass."

He was letting himself go, giving up a resistance which would be pointless. They were both naked and that seemed almost natural to him.

"Come and lie down here . . . No . . . Nearer . . . Don't move . . ."

He was thinking of the telephone booth, of the voices in the next-door room, of the words which the woman cried out in her paroxysm, and it was undoubtedly that which came to his rescue.

He saw nothing, observed nothing.

"Come on now . . . Ssh . . ."

He didn't want to think either. He was outside reality and time. It was not he, Emile Jovis, who, suddenly, seized with a kind of rage . . .

"What are you doing?"

If she was not truly afraid, she was surprised.

When he finally buried his face in the woman's shoulder, she murmured again:

"Well, you are a queer one! . . ."

He did not sit up at once, because he wanted to cry with the humiliation of it all. He too, at one moment, had just uttered, almost shouted, the words he had heard on the other side of the wall, and he might have been trying to destroy the woman in his arms who now looked drained of all blood.

She stole a glance at him and poured herself a drink. Perhaps she had been really afraid?

"What business do you run?"

He did not immediately understand.

"Do you think I run something?"

"You're surely not a mere employee."

He saw her, in the dressing room whose door she had left open.

"Aren't you coming?"

It was an ordeal washing in front of her.

"You must have an important position unless you run your own business."

"I don't run my own business."

"Well, I'm not curious."

"I'm the manager of a travel agency."

He added, adopting Monsieur Armand's word:

"In fact, I sell holidays."

He dressed rapidly, wondering how much he ought to give her. He hadn't the slightest idea. The luxuriousness of the studio impressed him.

"Whom should I pay for the champagne?"

"Leave what you like on the table."

"What about you?"

"It's all included."

He tried to calculate, turning his back on her to rummage in his wallet. First he took out two notes of a hundred francs each, added one, then another.

115

While she was standing in front of the mirror, he placed them on the table.

"Will you give me another bottle at the Carillon?"

He didn't dare say no. His watch showed ten minutes past one. In the ordinary course of events, according to what he had told Blanche, he should be back about two, but Blanche was far away, in another world, as unreal as their apartment.

The girl walked up and down the room two or three times as if she were making sure she hadn't forgotten anything; when he looked at the table again, the notes had disappeared.

"Come on. I've got to do my number again in about twenty minutes. Some evenings one's got to go on as often as five times. There are days when we have to turn people away. Monday's a dead day."

He followed her into the hallway and into the elevator, was out in the street again for a moment, and it was only when he plunged into the thick and vibrant atmosphere of the Carillon Doré that he began to be afraid.

It seemed to him that the cloakroom girl looked at him differently from when he had first arrived. Léon, over the tops of people's heads, looked as if he were picking him out, drawing him along, and, as none of the stools were free, he ousted two customers.

This surprised him. He looked for Farran, did not catch sight of him at once, but saw him return a little later, coming from outside.

Had he too been to the next-door studios? Had he taken one of the girls along—Alexa, for instance? No! Alexa was at the end of the bar, talking with a customer.

"A bottle of Mumm, Leon."

It all might have been prepared for in advance. Bucket and bottle appeared instantly on the bar top.

He did not want to drink. He wasn't drunk, even if he was

tending to imagine things. Why, for example, this feeling of insecurity?

Wasn't Adèle signaling to Léon? Wasn't he, in his turn, making a sign to Farran, who was now coming up?

He passed behind Jovis's back, then behind Irène, to whom he said as he pinched the back of her neck:

"Everything all right, sweetie?"

He didn't stop, but went and sat down where he had been in the first place, on the other side of Alexa. He seemed to know her companion, and all three of them began to chatter in an undertone. Because of the music, the other voices, and the noise of the dancing, it was impossible to hear what they were saying.

Why was Alexa looking at him as if there were something surprising about his clothes, or his behavior, or simply his presence?

Now and again she bent her head forward to hear better, but she didn't take her eyes off him and he would have sworn that they were talking about him.

"Chin-chin!"

Irène clinked her glass against his, as she had done in the room, and drank the champagne in one gulp.

"I'm going to get ready."

She left him alone at the bar, and he didn't know how to react.

Chapter Six

SUDDENLY he decided to leave. He seemed to be suffocating, to be overcome with giddiness. He had drunk too much, certainly, but it was above all because he was not used to drinking. It was creating a fluctuating connection between his brain and reality.

If he started to walk, he was sure he wouldn't stagger; he wasn't as far gone as that. He was equally capable of speaking without slurring his words. He knew where he was and what he was doing, and he had not forgotten the most minute detail of the evening's events.

On the contrary, his lucidness was doubled. Watching the faces around him, he felt he would be able to dig down into the depths of each individual and later conjure up the characteristics, the gestures, the states of mind of all the customers.

He had simply stayed too long, allowing the atmosphere of this strange night club to sweep over him and strip him of his means of defense.

He had followed Irène without a protest. Up there, in the studio, he had acted as they were expecting him to act. Almost too much so, since at one moment the girl had been frightened.

He said "they." He didn't say it, as he wasn't talking to anyone, but he thought it. These people, all around him, were of two kinds. There were those at the tables who were doing what "they" had decided to make them do and were now wearing paper hats, some of them blowing toy musical instruments, others throwing streamers or balls of colored cotton.

"They"—those were the others, from the cloakroom girl to the barman via the headwaiter, the waitresses and waiters, and perhaps also some of those who were leaning on the bar and contributed to the extras.

They hadn't lured him into the Carillon Doré. Not one among them was expecting to see him push open the door of the night club that particular Monday.

In their eyes, he could only have been some customer, an insignificant little man whom they would try to milk of as much money as possible.

Well, no! It hadn't happened like that. He had come in, had left his hat, had gone toward the bar instead of following the headwaiter.

At the bar there had been Farran, who glanced at him, just once. One glance which had been enough.

Had his neighbor at Fairview seen him, from his side of the terrace, when he was trying to keep out of his sight? When he had gone for a walk, in the afternoon, with his wife and son, hadn't Walter said to his parents:

"Look! That's him, my new friend Alain, with his father and mother"?

When he had seen him coming into view in Rue de Ponthieu, hadn't Farran realized that he knew everything?

Why, otherwise, this visit to a night club by a man who quite plainly was not used to such places?

His fright intensified. He did not want to wait for Irène to begin her number.

"How much do I owe you, barman?"

"You're not leaving already?"

Jovis could have sworn that Léon was looking for Farran to give him a signal. It was too bad if the drink was distorting reality. Jovis wanted to go. He wanted to go back to his wife and find her sleeping with her mouth half open, snoring faintly in that reassuring way, with his son curled up in his bed, without sheets or blankets.

This was his world. He had created it. He was responsible for it. Both of them needed him as much as he needed them.

He had already taken his wallet out of his pocket.

"The lady who owns the place wants you to have a bottle on the house," the barman pronounced, no longer the chubby little man he had been just now, adopting instead a disturbing manner.

Evidently he was party to the conspiracy. He had received instructions and was following them.

"Who is the lady who owns the place? Where is she?"

"Up there, in her apartment. It is a tradition to offer a bottle on the house to sympathetic new customers. Besides, Mademoiselle Irène would take it amiss if you didn't wait for her to come back. She'll be here in a moment. . . ."

Should he insist, or run away? He didn't dare to go, and returned his wallet to his pocket.

It seemed to him that Léon and Farran were exchanging significant glances. The band announced the next number with a roll on the drums, and the lights changed once again.

He pretended to be watching Irene, who was stripping as she moved up and down the floor, but it was another image which he saw, an image which he thought he had forgotten.

They were still on Rue des Francs-Bourgeois. It was sum-

120

mer, as now, because the window was wide open. All three of them were sitting at the table and the sun had just set, the air was taking on a blue tinge, it was not necessary to light the lamps.

Why does one remember one such moment in one's life rather than another? That particular moment Emile had lived through in all innocence, without realizing that he was in the act of registering it in his memory.

Alain was younger. He was about eight. He was pudgy at that time, and complained about having a fat behind which his friends laughed about. They were having dinner, at the oval table which was then covered not by a tablecloth but, for reasons of economy, by a red-checked piece of oilcloth.

Another window was open on the other side of the street, less than eight yards away, and two people were also having dinner at an oval table, in the middle of which there were a soup tureen and a piece of bread. They were the Bernards. They only knew them by sight. They had no children.

He was a policeman and they used to see him sometimes in mufti, sometimes in uniform, which impressed Alain. Particularly when he was about five or six.

"Is it a real revolver in his holster?"

"Yes."

"Is he allowed to shoot at people?"

"Only at criminals."

"The ones who kill or who steal?"

"As a rule they don't shoot at thieves."

"Why?"

In the two rooms separated by less than eight yards, the occupants spooned up their soup and wiped their lips with the same gestures. Madame Bernard was old before her time. Since the concierge had been ill, she had taken her place for most of the day in the lodge.

121

They were both talking, but one couldn't hear what they were saying. One merely felt that they were at peace, relaxed, relieved of the cares of the day.

That evening, at that moment, Jovis had thought there were hundreds of thousands of households, in Paris alone, having soup like that in a light which was turning blue in the dusk.

"What are you thinking about?" Blanche had asked him.

He had remained a long time without saying anything, lost in a dream.

"I'm thinking of the people opposite."

"Of the Bernards?"

"That woman hasn't much longer to live."

And yet she was still alive. It was the policeman who had been killed a few months later, intervening in a brawl.

Why did he conjure up the Bernards here, in such a different setting? His thoughts were meandering along in a complex way, passing first by Fairview, at the moment when they had driven up in front of the building, his wife and he, ahead of the moving van. The first face they had seen belonged to the invalid with the bloodshot eyes and the polished cranium, leaning out of a window on the third floor.

He remembered how he had felt then. It had not been exactly disappointment, but he had been vexed at not feeling more enthusiastic, and the rest of the day had passed rather as if in limbo.

He had had trouble in convincing himself that everything was real, that this apartment belonged to him, more precisely would belong to him when he had finished paying the installments.

How many years would they live there? In six years, in eight years, in ten years, Alain would leave them to get married or to work somewhere else. They would stay, the two of them, like the Bernards on Rue des Francs-Bourgeois.

Had he been right to? . . .

He hadn't been sure, the first day at Fairview, or the second either. Had he been so sure the day before, when they had been walking, the three of them, along the dusty road and had discovered a steeple, a hamlet, real peasants playing cards in the cool of a country bistro?

He had looked at Blanche, seeking to read some regret in her face.

On Rue des Francs-Bourgeois, they had been surrounded by modest, humdrum people leading a life which was drab but uncomplicated. They accepted their mediocrity without rebelling against it, as they accepted their setbacks, their illnesses, the infirmities of old age.

Blanche had not said anything when she discovered that there was no church. As a rule, she went to Mass on Sundays. When they had decided to leave early for the country, she had rushed to the six o'clock morning service at St. Paul's and a picnic lunch was ready by the time her two men had got up.

Since she was devout, wasn't she angry with her husband for not believing as well? She never spoke about it, made no allusion to God or to religion.

He was convinced that she was waiting, as she prayed for him, for the day when he would see the light.

If she had married a sinner, at least she had managed to be married in church.

"If we don't, my aunt won't give her consent, and she's my guardian."

Blanche had only been nineteen then. Her aunt went to the first morning Mass and to communion every day. She was one of the rare people at Kremlin-Bicêtre still to go to the evening service.

"On condition that it's early and no one is invited to the church," Emile's father, resolutely atheist, had grumbled.

Blanche's witness had been a friend of the aunt's, and Emile had asked a colleague to be his after he had made sure that he had been baptized.

Alain had been baptized too.

"And deliver us from evil . . ."

Why these memories, suddenly, in surroundings so unpropitious to this kind of thought?

Evil. Good. For Blanche, it was cut and dried. She was sure of herself and it was this no doubt which gave her her serenity.

She did not advertise her convictions. If there was a bronze statue of Christ in the house, it was not on the wall, but in a drawer, with her ribbons, reels of cotton, and odds and ends of material which might come in useful one day.

If, before taking her first mouthful of food, she slightly moved her lips as she recited to herself the benedicite, it was barely noticeable.

In front of him, Irène was removing her briefs, facing the spectators, and half an hour earlier Emile had been buried in her flesh.

Viciously. . . . Like Farran. . . . He hadn't done it on purpose. . . . Now he wondered where this sudden desire to destroy her had come from. . . . Was it in imitation? Had the voices on the other side of the wall awakened in him instincts which he didn't suspect he had or which had been snuffed out by long cohabitation with Blanche? . . .

"Cheers! . . . Keep drinking while the champagne is still fresh. . . ."

And, as the lights went up again, the barman added:

"She'll be along right away. . . ."

That story of the owner offering free champagne to new customers was nonsense. It was a little like the Barillon Travel Agency paying the cost of a stay at Nice for all those coming in for the first time.

They were treating him like a fool, were hardly bothering to hide the game they were playing.

What were they waiting for him to do?

"Chin-chin!"

He drained his glass in one gulp. He wanted to urinate. Would they let him leave the bar? He slid from his stool, felt a moment of giddiness, and made for the little door against which Farran had recently been leaning. He read the word "Toilets" on it. He must keep his eyes fixed on it, make certain that he didn't end up somewhere else.

On the way, he collided with a chair occupied by a brunette.

"I beg your pardon."

Pardon for what? What could one ask pardon for here? Everything was allowed, even stripping naked!

He laughed derisively. They thought they had him already, but he was as cunning as they were. What was worrying Farran was everything that he had told his wife in the course of the preceding nights.

How had they found out that Emile had heard?

It was simple enough, for God's sake! If the partition was thin enough to let through sounds in one direction, it would let them through inevitably in the other direction.

So Farran, or his wife, or both of them, had heard them, Blanche and him, when they were talking in their bedroom.

Their remarks must have seemed naïve, ridiculous.

"Do you realize, Jean?"

For Farran's Christian name was Jean, he remembered, he remembered everything, he had an extraordinary memory, so much so that Monsieur Armand had congratulated him on it many times.

"Yes . . ." an anxious Farran must have muttered.

"If they've heard what I tell you while we're making love . . ."

125

That amused her all right. She would probably have carried on and cried out in the same way if the wall had not existed. Who knows? That might have excited her even more.

He looked at himself in the washroom mirror and saw something awry in his face, a look he did not know, a sarcastic expression.

He washed his hands carefully, as if this gesture had enormous importance, drying them on a roller towel on which he found a piece which was tolerably dry.

He lit a cigarette, still standing in front of the mirror.

It wasn't true that he was frightened. He was capable of holding his own against them. In spite of what had happened with Irène, he was an honorable man and he had a conscience. They wouldn't make him say what he didn't want to say, champagne or no champagne.

Wasn't he engaged in spending in one night enough money to buy Alain his motor scooter, even enough for two?

Wasn't it his right, after all? Hasn't everyone the right, once in his life, to do something special, something which lifts him out of the usual routine?

He had always worked desperately hard. That no one could deny. And, if he had got to where he was, it was thanks to his energy, to his evening courses, to his self-sacrifice.

Exactly, to his self-sacrifice! He was no saint. He had had temptations, like everyone, and he was well aware, when he had married Blanche, that she was not a pretty woman.

He also foresaw that she would quickly fade, and that she would not provide him with certain pleasures which he preferred not to specify but which any man may dream about.

Someone came in, while he looked as if he were talking to himself in front of the mirror, and he left the washroom, finding himself back in the heat, in the music, in a fog from which emerged pink heads and the colorful splashes made by the women's dresses.

126

Where was Farran? Was he worried about his long absence?

This idea made him smile. It was he, Jovis, who had got his neighbor. He would only have to ask him, for instance:

"By the way, where is Little Louis?"

Because it wasn't only the hysterical paroxysms that had been heard on the other side of the wall. There were also the cars.

Had Farran thought about it? The cars which Little Louis had "lifted"? Didn't the word say only too well what it meant?

Well, what possible good could it do them, one bottle more or less? It must be intended to coax him along, to draw him onto their side. Emile had been wrong to give so much money to Irène. If things had gone so smoothly, it was because she had had her instructions.

She would have slept with him as easily as winking.

She was there, at the bar, and this time Alexa was occupying a stool next to her.

"No need to introduce you. You've seen her dance. She's our biggest star."

"Stop it!" the other girl said, in the same raucous voice as Farran's wife. "Tell me, Irène insists you're great."

"At what?"

"Do you hear that, Irène? He doesn't understand!"

He did understand and he was now in a favorable position.

"Chin-chin!"

He had never before heard these two words so often, but they no longer shocked him by their vulgarity. He replied:

"Chin-chin!"

Both the girls were drinking, and Alexa had placed a hot hand on his knee.

"I hope you'll come again. Have you been to Tahiti?"

"No."

"I went last year, with a club. When you leave, they put

garlands around your neck made of hibiscus flowers. When the boat is at a distance, you throw the flowers into the water and if they float this means that you will return. . . .

"Here it's the same thing, when Léon offers someone a bottle on the house."

He could no longer see Farran. He didn't know what time it was, and didn't dare look at his wrist watch.

"Do you travel a lot?" asked Alexa, keeping up her endless chatter.

And Irène continued interposing herself:

"He sells trips. How did you put it just now? Ah, yes, it's more amusing. He's a dealer in holidays."

"I'm in a travel agency."

"The manager!" Irène was more precise.

"Doesn't that make you want to go off on holiday too?"

"Not at the same time as the others. For us, it's the height of the season."

"For us as well."

He saw himself in the mirror behind the bottles, his face more and more strange, his eyes shining, his color heightened. What was he doing here showing off before the two women and strutting about like a peacock? Didn't he know that it was all phony, that everything had been arranged in advance?

The funniest thing of all would be if they suggested that he should buy a second-hand car, a car "lifted" by Little Louis!

. . . but deliver us from evil, Amen . . .

The words came back to him, as in the catechism.

. . . which art in heaven . . . lead us not into temptation . . .

Had he succumbed? Had he put up a sufficient defense against the evil spirit? He laughed derisively, no longer

128

knowing whether he was blaspheming or whether he really believed in good and evil.

Evil, *the evil one,* that was Farran, a fair-haired devil, well-built, bare-chested, flat-stomached, dressed in shorts on his terrace, lighting a cigarette with a gold lighter . . .

Jovis had bested him! . . . He had found him again . . . Already he had made love with one of his girls, the one whom his neighbor had nonchalantly announced he had taken in the telephone booth.

"By the way, is there a telephone booth here?"

"Do you want to call your wife?"

"First, I haven't said I was going to telephone anyone . . . Secondly, I only asked whether such a thing exists . . . Thirdly, a telephone booth has other uses besides making telephone calls . . ."

Bang! He looked Irène straight in the eyes as he said that, but as the girl didn't flinch, he added:

"Just as a bed is for more things than sleeping . . ."

Another hit, wasn't it? Had she understood, this time?

He was rid of it. Rid of the thought that either of them had guessed. They thought that he was talking like that because he had drunk a few glasses of champagne, without realizing what was essential to him about the evening. *Essential!* He was thinking certain words in capital letters.

He had cut away a mooring line. He had got rid of . . . It wasn't easy to explain, but he felt free. Free and strong.

Crap, that was the word! Good, evil, all crap, don't you understand?

He didn't say it to them. He saw the barman's face, his eyes never leaving him, taking advantage of the moments when he turned his head away to refill his glass. There was a third bottle on the bar. Then what?

Had Blanche the right to grudge him this? Hadn't he been

129

a model husband and oughtn't she to thank him for having chosen her out of thousands, out of tens of thousands, out of hundreds of thousands of other women?

Could she have stripped in the middle of a night club, and displayed her breasts, her stomach, her buttocks?

No! Well, then?

He had slept with Irène, who knew all about it and who had confided in her pal Alexa that he was *extraordinary*.

Nor could Alain reproach him with anything. There wouldn't have been any Alain if Jovis hadn't wanted it.

. . . but deliver us . . .

"Where is he?" he suddenly queried, looking around as if he had remembered an urgent engagement.

"Who?"

"The tall fair man who was sitting at the end of the bar just now."

"I suppose he's left."

"Don't either of you know him?"

Alexa was the only one to reply.

"I know him as I know the customers, no more no less. So many come here . . ."

"Does he come here often?"

She was lying and it amused him to force her into lies.

"Now and then . . ."

She had taken her hand away from Emile's thigh and was watching him with a certain mistrust.

"Not every night?"

"You've got some funny ideas, my pet. What makes you think that he comes every night?"

"I don't know. I thought . . ."

"Thought what?"

"That he was something like the owner."

"The owner's a woman, Madame Porchet. She lives on the

mezzanine floor and doesn't come down any more since she lost a leg in a car accident."

"Is she an old woman?"

"Ten years ago she was the best striptease artist in Paris."

"How did she get to be the owner?"

"By marrying the man who owned it then, Fernand Porchet."

"And what happened to Fernand Porchet?"

"He's dead."

"How?"

He was playing at getting her with her back to the wall. He knew certain things and she didn't know that he knew.

"In an accident."

"Car?"

"No. A gun."

"Did he commit suicide?"

"He didn't do it himself."

This gave him a jolt, and he emptied his glass of champagne.

"And the others?"

Neither of them understood the point of his question.

"Which others? What are you talking about?"

He was becoming rash, but he felt he was invincible. They couldn't do a thing to him. He was free, and able to face them out.

"All the others, for God's sake! The gang!"

He pointed to Léon, then to the headwaiter, the waiters, and even the cloakroom girl.

Léon didn't flinch but looked at the two women insistently as if to give them their instructions. He was certainly not the boss. He didn't have the brains. Farran, on the other hand, had the brains for a boss. But Léon must be something important and secure, like an adjutant.

"You're funny!"

"Why shouldn't I be funny? Didn't I tell you that I sold holidays? They're gay things, holidays! I'm on holiday and I'm gay. . . ."

It was his turn to place his hand on Alexa's thigh and tell her in tones of conviction:

"Tomorrow, I'll be back, and it'll be you I'll have fun with."

There! It was the first time he had used this phrase, and he hadn't got there so easily.

"I already know what you'll do to me, what you'll ask me to do to you. And I know how you'll react."

She wasn't smiling so naturally any more, and he had the impression that he was frightening her a bit.

Still, he decided to go further, much further. He'd had enough of an honest little man's timidity. That was finished. *Fin-ished.*

"I'll tell you what you'll ask me to do. Let me whisper in your ear . . ."

And he repeated, in an undertone, the words he had heard coming from his neighbor's mouth.

"That astonishes you, doesn't it?"

She looked at the barman, and he moved away as if to serve other customers. Actually, he left the bar and made his way toward the little door by the washroom.

"I bet he's off to fetch Farran!"

"Who did you say?"

"I said Farran."

"Who's he? Someone you know?"

He looked at them, malicious, laughing and frightened at the same time. He hadn't wanted to go so far. He had forgotten that he was not supposed to know.

"And what about you?"

132

"Here we don't usually ask customers their names. Only their Christian names. What's your Christian name?"

"Emile."

Irène had withdrawn into the background, leaving the direction of operations to Alexa. The latter said almost without sarcasm:

"I'd have bet on that."

"Why?"

"Because it suits you."

He guessed in a confused way that she was making fun of him, and this annoyed him.

"You forget that I don't know any more about you than you do about me. Perhaps I am called Emile, but I'm not . . ."

He stopped short. Only now did he notice the barman's absence. More exactly, he saw him come into view, near the little door, when he still thought he was behind him.

"Where's he coming from, that man?"

"Who are you talking about?"

"Léon."

"I expect from the washroom."

"No. He came out of the other door. Where does it lead to, that way out?"

"Into the wings. We must have a place to change, to put the props, and somewhere else for the stocks of bottles."

He looked all around the room and his anxiety increased. He established the fact that most of the customers had gone, that there were only three couples still at their tables, and that the band was putting away its instruments.

This did not sober him up completely, but he felt less sure of himself. Suddenly he was eager to be outside, to get out of the trap.

For it was a trap in which he was beginning to struggle.

"What do I owe you, barman?"

"You're not going off like that when the ladies haven't finished their drinks."

He looked at Alexa and Irène in turn, no longer seeing them as before. They were not exactly alike, but the smiles on their lips were twisted, their features set, almost menacing.

Perhaps it was his imagination.

"Let them finish them."

Irène seemed to have understood some sort of signal made by the barman.

"I'll tell you something, darling. You were talking just now of coming back tomorrow for Alexa. Tomorrow is her day off. She told me just now that she felt like . . . you understand? We'll have another bottle, all very nicely, then all three of us'll go next door . . ."

He held on to the bar, because he seemed to make the stool wobble. Frowning, he made an effort to understand. Why did they want to take him off to a studio in the next-door house?

"Is it a trap?" he asked in a thick voice.

Léon, without waiting for his answer, had opened a bottle and was filling the glasses.

"What trap? Why would we set a trap for you? We both of us feel like having fun with you . . ."

. . . but deliver us . . .

No! He had had enough of that endlessly repeated phrase.

"Why did you go into the wings, you?" he suddenly asked, turning toward the barman.

"To tell the owner that everything was in order."

"She's up there, the owner."

"There's an intercom telephone."

"Who decided to stop the music?"

"No one. The band knows when it has to play and when

it hasn't. No one was listening any more, and there are no more people dancing."

One of the three couples was making its way toward the exit. Two couples left and there remained only one solitary person at the bar, an Englishman dozing over his glass of whisky and now and then calling Léon to fill it up.

"Chin-chin!"

No! No more *chin-chin!* Neither *chin-chin* nor *deliver us from evil.*

He had enough trouble finding his bearings as it was. He no longer even knew how it had started. It was evidently his fault. It was always his fault. Blanche never made a decision. She did what he wanted. She was a submissive wife. *Submissive!*

Hadn't Irène, just now, in the studio, been just as submissive? There's nothing easier. And Alain was submissive. If he was disobedient, it was slyly, so that his father could not tell. He was, that was certain. Perhaps that very day he had confided to his schoolmates:

"Yesterday, while we were out for a walk, I put on an act —someone who was bored and who had been sacrificed because of the move. It worked. I'm getting my scooter."

They were all cheating. Everyone cheated. Jovis himself was engaged in passing off the biggest cheat of his life.

He would finish the bottle with the two girls, since he had to. If he didn't, they would be capable of stopping him from leaving their night club. God knows who was behind the mysterious little door.

And there was another couple leaving. Only one was left, a pair of lovers kissing. The man was brazenly kneading his companion's breasts as if they were alone together.

There, the bottle was finished. . . .

Ah! yes. . . . He remembered. . . . He would leave quietly with Alexa and Irène. . . .

Perhaps it wouldn't have been a bad idea to go off to the studio, all three of them. All three naked!

But he mustn't. It was another trap. Once he was in the street, he would swallow a great mouthful of air and be off.

There were other night clubs nearby, restaurants still open. He would run if necessary and no one would dare to rush off in pursuit. Once he was on the Champs-Elysées he would only have to go and pick up his car. . . .

The proof that he was not as drunk as all that was that he remembered perfectly well the place where he had left the car. In the underground garage on Avenue George V. He would have to drive slowly, trying not to make mistakes because, if a policeman or a patrol car made him stop, he might possibly be put through the alcohol test . . . the breath-alyzer . . . A word like that! A difficult word, particularly tonight!

A sudden thought chilled him.

Supposing Farran really was in the wings, as he had suspected for some time? Supposing Farran followed him in his red sports car?

On the throughway Jovis would be running no risk, because of the lights and the traffic. But when he turned right, when he took the empty road to Fairview and passed under the railway bridge?

One read stories like that in the papers. One saw them on television.

They were afraid of him, that was certain. How many of them were there in this racket? There was Little Louis, who "lifted" the cars. Then they had to change the license plates and the registration card. Or else there was someone in the civil service who trafficked in registration cards, or an expert who manufactured false ones.

There was a garage somewhere.

"What's the matter?"

"Nothing. It's hot."

"Drink up. The champagne will refresh you."

He looked at her with a kind of pained irony. Fate had poked fun at him. If something was going to happen to him tonight, he would regret at the final moment having picked Irène. For actually it had been pure chance.

He could have had, when he came in, a stool next to Alexa. He would have sat down. She would have behaved like her friend, because that was the way they all behaved. Then it would have been Alexa with whom he would have gone to the studio next door.

And Alexa was exactly the kind of woman he had dreamed all his life of possessing at least once.

On the face of it, he still could. They had suggested that all three of them should go to the "studio."

But it wasn't true. It was pointless having any illusions. Everything around him had changed. The last couple had gone. Only his own hat remained hanging in the cloakroom, and the young girl had disappeared. The Englishman as well.

The lighting was no longer tangerine-colored, but a harsh white, and two old women were starting to sweep up the streamers and the multicolored balls.

Léon was not a jovial barman, a plump man smiling blandly. His eyes were cold, and he was filling the glasses as if he were ordering Jovis to drink.

What was forcing him, after all?

"No!"

He was stupefied to hear his voice reverberate in the silence, because he had imagined that he was thinking only in the innermost recess of his heart.

"Who are you saying no to?"

He looked at them, and they were more and more distorted, they were harder and harder, closing in on him as if to prevent him from running away.

137

"I don't know. I was thinking . . ."

"What of?"

"Of . . . of my wife. . . ."

He was inventing, trying to gain time. Above all he must not fall down. If he fell while he was getting down from the stool, he would be at their mercy.

He knew, now, when it had started. The move! Because it had not been a real move. It had been a betrayal. He had betrayed them all by running away.

It hadn't been only the wallpaper which irritated him, but the people on Rue des Francs-Bourgeois.

Who had said:

"Pride goeth before a fall"?

It didn't matter. He had betrayed them, his father, the policeman across the way, his wife who had replaced the concierge—that's right, the concierge had died—and also poor Blanche, whom he had transplanted as if she were a geranium plant.

It was funny thinking of Blanche as a geranium. A geranium also is peaceable, humble, reassuring, and indistinguishable from another geranium. There are hundreds of thousands around just as there are hundreds of thousands of Blanches whom one cannot tell apart when they hug the walls on their way to do the shopping or when they go to early Mass.

He had betrayed Alain, too, now that he had only Walter as a friend and he would have to leave the Lycée Charlemagne and go every morning to the school at Villejuif.

He was thinking fast. It didn't stop him from listening to the two women. Irène was describing the dress she would wear in her next number and the slower way she would strip.

"I know I'm doing it wrong. I'm going too fast. I can't stop it."

He was just about to fall asleep, like the Englishman. He gave a start.

"The check!" he cried too loudly, as if his voice were still covered by the din of the band.

"Pay tomorrow, or another day."

"What does that mean?"

He was annoyed and looked hard at Léon.

"Haven't I the right to pay? And why, may I ask? Isn't my money as good as anyone else's?"

Alexa took him by the arm and made him get down off his stool.

"Come on, darling."

He shrugged her off.

"One moment. Not before . . ."

He pulled his wallet from his pocket, and took out some hundred-franc notes, three, four, perhaps five. He had taken care to provide himself before going out with a sum of money he was not used to carrying on him.

"There! If it's not enough, say so!"

"Thank you, sir."

"Why didn't he want me to pay?"

"To give you a present."

"A present?"

"Because he likes you, of course! Don't worry about that any more. Come on. We'll go and have fun . . ."

Each of the girls took one of his arms and he repeated to himself:

"We'll go and have some fun."

139

Chapter Seven

HE was not surprised. He was ready for anything. He felt that he had become incredibly clear-sighted, and it seemed to him that he had discovered the secret of mankind and the universe.

It gave him a bitterly ironic feeling, aimed just as much at himself as at the others.

"There we are. Watch out for the step."

They were supporting him. Just a second earlier both of them were at his sides. Then, a moment later, without any transition, he was standing alone in the middle of the sidewalk.

It was obviously a joke. He had never believed that they were going to take him to the studio and that all three of them would undress.

They were cheating him. Right from the start. He wasn't going to take it lying down. Less than fifty yards away there was another night club, its name standing out in the darkness in purple lights. He made an effort to read it. The letters overlapped. It was La Tige, or Le Tigre.

A doorman in a gray waistcoat, at the entrance, was chatting with a policeman. Apart from them, the street was empty.

Was it because of the policeman that the two women had let him go? He turned around to see what had happened to them. They were no longer there. Perhaps they had gone back into the Carillon? Or else had they gone on toward the head of the street and were too far away to be seen?

How would it all end for him? The die was cast. Come what may, he was not afraid. He had always stuck by his responsibilities, like a man. No one could pretend that he wasn't a man.

The difficulty was to keep his balance, now that they were no longer there to hold him up, and every now and then his shoulder knocked against the wall.

Because of the policeman, he must walk straight. The policeman had made them afraid, but he wasn't going to make him afraid. He had nothing to reproach himself for. Perhaps he was damned, if Blanche's Hell existed, but he had nothing to be ashamed of.

A man has the right, once in his lifetime, to make love to a woman other than his wife. He hadn't even asked for it. It was she who had organized the whole thing.

Should he say as he passed:

"Good evening, officer"?

No. That would smack of provocation.

And if he said:

"At the Carillon there's a man called Farran and his gang. A certain Little Louis lifts the cars, and then, when a customer is drunk, Alexa . . . Listen to me . . . Perhaps I'm drunk too, but I know what I'm saying. . . . Alexa, that's the dark one, she's got a body . . ."

A body like what? Sinuous! That's it. It's difficult to describe a body, and he had found the word: sinuous! And a

141

mouth . . . For the mouth, he did not find the right word, but anyone would understand.

In short, he had the chance to get them all in the soup. They would be arrested. They would be taken off to prison.

Even so, he went past between the two men without saying a word, and they paid no attention to him.

Shouldn't the policeman have questioned him? Hadn't he understood, just by looking at him, that something out of the ordinary was going on? Jovis had not been drunk once in his life, before this. No, officer, not even the day when they celebrated my promotion at the Place de la Bastille office.

His colleagues had offered him champagne. Not real champagne. Sparkling wine. Monsieur Armand had been quite carried away and had delivered a speech about the one big family they were all a part of and which would flourish and multiply for the greater benefit of . . .

It was idiotic! Policemen have no intuition. All they're good at is regulating the traffic. The real work is done by the others, by those who are dressed like everybody else and whom one would never recognize.

If there had been one of those in front of him now . . .

Where was he? On Rue de Ponthieu, yes . . . He must get off this street, which was not leading him toward his car . . . It was parked in the underground garage on Avenue George V . . .

To get there, he must find his way out of this downhill slit where he couldn't see a single person, and there were no lights besides the lampposts.

He must find a way out to take him to the left, toward the Champs-Elysées, where Monsieur Armand was in charge of the agency which seemed to be made exclusively of glass. Pity that it wasn't open at night. He would have gone and told him, Monsieur Armand . . .

Had they perhaps poisoned him? He managed to pull his handkerchief out of his pocket to mop his forehead, which was dripping with sweat.

In any case, they would put up a defense. He knew too much about them. He had let on to Alexa and Irène.

It was curious. He could not manage to convince himself that he had slept with Irène. Wouldn't something like that have left some trace? After it was over, she had been the same as before, as if nothing had happened between them.

He knew too much about them. He could get them all arrested. That was not his intention. He was not—what did they call it?—a stool pigeon . . .

If they left him alone, he, for his part, wouldn't get mixed up in what they were doing. One stolen car more or less . . .

The only thing was that they didn't know that. And Léon, the barman, had watched him with the eye of a serpent. Then he had gone into the wings where Farran was hiding.

Farran was the boss. He had the air of a boss.

What were they going to do? They had let him leave the Carillon Doré. Perhaps because, inside, they wouldn't have known how to get rid of his body.

A dead body is a cumbersome thing. It is practically always because of the body that criminals are caught. . . .

He was walking. He was floating. He seemed to step off the sidewalk and miraculously to step onto it again.

He remembered everything. Not in the proper sequence, of course. Good and evil, for God's sake . . . That was nothing but a load of crap!

What would happen if he died tonight without returning to Fairview? Fairview! A name like a pseudonym. A village, a borough, a small town, they didn't have names like that. Even the name was enough to show how faked the whole thing was.

He had been walking, but not for a long time. Since the first day, when they had arrived a bit ahead of the furniture . . .

Would his wife and son understand how he had spent the last night of his life?

Who would tell them? Not Léon, who would hardly boast of forcing him to drink. Not the girls, who were in the plot. The cloakroom girl? She seemed more decent than the others and watched what was going on with indifference and at a safe distance.

Blanche would know, one way or another. There was no reason for him to be killed in the Champs-Elysées district when he was supposed to be at Orly. He might even have been home a long time now, and suddenly his forehead again broke out in a terrible sweat.

He hadn't thought of that. He had said that he would be back at two in the morning at the latest. Since it was the first time, in fifteen years of married life, that he was away for part of the night, Blanche would probably not have gone to bed. She was quite capable of waiting up for him.

Then, seeing the hours go past . . .

What time was it?

"What time is it?" he shouted into the emptiness of the night, forgetting that he had a watch on his wrist.

Wouldn't it soon be dawn? She would telephone the airport. She would ask:

"Did the charter plane leave long ago?"

So she knew now that there had been no charter plane. He had lied to her. What proof was there that it was the first time in fifteen years?

No one has the right to fill the head of a single man with so many worries. A street intersected Rue de Ponthieu and he must take the right turn. Once he was on the Champs-

Elysées, he would be safe. It was Rue La Boétie. There was a car parked, quite far away, near Saint-Philippe-du-Roule, but it wasn't a red convertible.

Wait a moment! He hadn't seen Farran's red car when he left the night club. Perhaps after all he had gone off after giving his instructions. A boss doesn't bother about details, he doesn't participate in their execution.

Who knows whether he wasn't back in his apartment, making his wife cry out that no one would hear them any longer from the other side of the wall?

It was really there that it had all started . . .

But what was the use? He was walking . . . He must go on walking . . . Another forty or so yards and he would be on the wide sidewalk of the Champs-Elysées.

The car, behind him, had started up. It had a powerful engine, which made the same noise as the red car.

He nearly turned around, as the car was approaching very fast, but it seemed to him that he shouldn't do so. The best thing was to run. Perhaps he would reach the corner in time . . .

Alone on the sidewalk, he must look like a puppet and he . . .

He heard the noise of a burst of gunfire, as if it came from a movie or on television. It gave him a shock. He came to a standstill, hesitating, filled with a sensation of just having been cut in two.

He wasn't dead. He wasn't ill. He was still on his feet.

No. He wasn't still on his feet. His head was bumping hard against the stones of the sidewalk, and it was in his head that he felt the pain.

Even so, he held both his hands to his stomach.

Had the policeman, on Rue de Ponthieu . . . Blanche would think he was in Hell . . . He had foreseen everything

. . . He felt quite lucid . . . She would think he was in Hell . . . And if she were right? . . . If there were really a Hell? . . .

All his life, he had . . .

It was tiring. Why did they leave him all alone? It was flowing, all hot. Not from his head.

And then he felt what seemed like dagger thrusts in his stomach.

"I'm so sorry . . ."

The man bending over him—an enormous head, a huge nose, like something in a nightmare—was repeating:

"Where are you hurt?"

"I didn't want . . ."

There! The policeman was there as well, and, a little farther away, a woman's legs.

"I didn't want to bother you . . ."

He would have liked to smile at them. Could he manage it? Could he . . .

It was too late. He couldn't see anything any more. He was no longer with the others. He heard the sound of a whistle, an engine, voices, but that didn't concern him.

Did he cry out? It's not right to cry out in the street in the middle of the night.

"Why are these people . . ."

They were talking. They were pricking him in the arm. Or perhaps it was in the thigh, he no longer knew.

She would wear mourning. She would not need to buy a new dress because she already had a black dress which she wore to go to Mass.

She would become a little old woman. He had always thought that she was born to become a little old woman. A widow, like the many widows on Rue des Francs-Bourgeois.

Perhaps she would end up as a housekeeper?

She would get money from the insurance policy.

He had stopped crying out, he was no longer in pain. He was beginning to fall asleep. They were shaking him. He wondered why they were shaking him instead of leaving him in peace.

What would they tell Alain? He had neglected to buy him his scooter and his son would never forgive him. It was too late now. They couldn't go on living at Fair . . . Fairwhat . . . The ridiculous name which had spoiled everything . . .

"Is he dead, Doctor?"

It was strange hearing, very clearly, that question.

"Not yet."

Well then, why were they stopping him from breathing? They were stuffing something over his nose and pressing down hard.

They would have to be at the trial, she in black, Alain in his best brown suit, but they would sew a black band on the sleeve.

"The widow and her son . . ."

The police take their time, but they always get there in the end. There they were lined up in the box, Farran in the middle, and Léon, the barman, Alexa . . .

He didn't like the smell. He didn't like it at all, no not at all, what they were doing to him, making the most of . . .

A brilliant idea . . . He was sure he had a brilliant idea . . . Let them give him a few seconds, let them allow him to speak instead of closing his mouth with something which smelled so bad . . .

Rue des Francs-Bourgeois . . . Let them just repeat those words to his wife . . .

Blanche would understand at once . . . Their apartment was perhaps not yet rented . . .

As they used to be . . .

He could have wept . . .

As they used to be, but without him . . .

The rent wasn't high . . . Perhaps Monsieur Armand would make a gesture . . . They mustn't forget the insurance policy, which he had always paid to the last penny . . .

They mustn't believe everything that . . .

"Sor . . . Sor . . ."

There was a powerful light in front of his eyes, a light as powerful as Hell.

"Sorry . . ."

Epalinges, June 27, 1967